Maigret
Goes
Home

Also by Georges Simenon
in Thorndike Large Print ®

The Murderer
Maigret at the Gai-Moulin
Maigret and the Gangsters

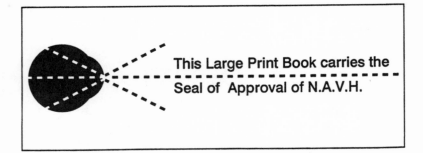

This Large Print Book carries the
Seal of Approval of N.A.V.H.

Maigret Goes Home

Georges Simenon

Translated by Robert Baldick

Thorndike Press • Thorndike, Maine

Library of Congress Cataloging in Publication Data:

Simenon, Georges, 1903-
    Maigret goes home / Georges Simenon ; translated by
Robert Baldick.
    p.   cm.
    ISBN 1-56054-529-1 (alk. paper : lg. print)
    1. Large type books. I. Title.
[PQ2637.I53A713   1993]   92-32617
843'.912—dc20   CIP

Thorndike Large Print® All-Time Favorites Series edition
published in 1993 by arrangement with Harcourt Brace
Jovanovich, Inc.

Cover design by James B. Murray.

The tree indicium is a trademark of Thorndike Press.

This book is printed on acid-free, high opacity paper. ∞

Maigret
Goes
Home

— 1 —
The Little Girl with the Squint

There was a timid scratching at the door, the sound of an object being put on the floor, a furtive voice:

"It's half past five! The first bell for All Souls' Day Mass has just been rung. . . ."

Maigret raised himself on his elbows, making the mattress creak, and while he was looking in astonishment at the skylight cut in the sloping roof, the voice went on:

"Are you taking Communion?"

By now Chief Inspector Maigret was out of bed, standing barefoot on the icy floor. He walked toward the door, which was closed with a piece of string wound around a couple of nails. There was the sound of footsteps hurrying away. When he looked out into the hallway, he was just in time to catch sight of the figure of a woman in a bed jacket and a white petticoat.

He picked up the jug of hot water Marie Tatin had brought him, closed his door, and looked for a piece of mirror in front of which he could shave.

The candle had only a few minutes of life left. Outside the skylight, it was still night, a cold night in early winter. A few dead leaves were clinging to the branches of the poplars in the marketplace.

Maigret could stand up only in the middle of the attic, because of the double slope of the roof. He was cold. A thin draft, the source of which he had been unable to trace, chilled the back of his neck.

It was precisely this quality of coldness that disturbed him, by plunging him into an atmosphere he thought he had forgotten.

The first bell for Mass . . . The bell ringing out over the sleeping village . . . When he was a boy, Maigret did not usually get up so early. He would wait for the second bell, because in those days he did not need to shave. Did he so much as wash his face?

Nobody brought him any hot water. Sometimes the water was frozen in the jug. Soon afterward his shoes would be clattering along the frozen road.

Now, while he was getting dressed, he could hear Marie Tatin coming and going in the main room of the inn, rattling the grate of the stove, moving crockery about, and turning the handle of the coffee mill.

He put on his jacket, his overcoat. Before going out, he removed from his wallet a piece of paper with an official slip pinned to it bearing the words:

MUNICIPAL POLICE OF MOULINS
Communicated for information and possible action to the Police Judiciaire in Paris:

Then a sheet of lined paper with laborious handwriting:

This is to tell you that a crime will be committed in the church at Saint-Fiacre during the first Mass on All Souls' Day.

The sheet of paper had lain around for several days in the offices of the Quai des Orfèvres. Maigret had noticed it by accident, and had asked in surprise:

"Is that the Saint-Fiacre near Matignon?"

"Probably, since it was sent to us by Moulins."

And Maigret had put the piece of paper in his pocket. Saint-Fiacre, Matignon, Moulins: words more familiar to him than almost any others.

He had been born in Saint-Fiacre, where his father had been the estate manager of the chateau for many years. The last time he had gone there had, in fact, been after the death

9

of his father, who had been buried in the little graveyard behind the church.

. . . a crime will be committed . . . during the first Mass . . .

Maigret had arrived the day before. He had taken a room at the only inn in the village: Marie Tatin's. She had not recognized him, but he had known her because of her eyes. The little girl with the squint, as they used to call her. A puny little girl who had become an even skinnier old maid, squinting more and more, and endlessly bustling about the bar, the kitchen, and the yard, where she kept rabbits and hens.

The chief inspector went downstairs. The ground-floor rooms were lit by oil lamps. A table was laid in one corner. There was coarse gray bread, a smell of coffee with chicory, and boiling milk.

"You're wrong not to take Communion on a day like today. Especially seeing that you're taking the trouble to go to the first Mass. . . . Heavens! That's the second bell ringing already!"

The voice of the bell was faint. Footsteps could be heard on the road. Marie Tatin fled into her kitchen to put on her black dress, her cotton gloves, and her little hat, which her bun prevented from staying on straight.

"I'll leave you to finish your breakfast. . . . You'll lock the door, won't you?"

"No, wait! I'm ready."

She was embarrassed to be walking with a man. A man who came from Paris! She trotted along, a small bent figure, in the cold morning air. Some dead leaves were fluttering about on the ground. The crisp sound they made showed that there had been a frost during the night.

There were other shadowy figures converging on the dimly shining doorway of the church. The bell was still ringing. There were lights in the windows of some low-built houses: people dressing in a hurry for the first Mass.

Maigret rediscovered other impressions from his childhood: the cold, the eyes smarting, the tips of the fingers frozen, a lingering taste of coffee in the mouth. Then, on going into the church, a wave of warm air, of soft light; the smell of the tapers and the incense.

"Excuse me, will you? . . . I've got my own prayer stool," she said.

And Maigret recognized the black chair with the red velvet armrest of old Madame Tatin, the mother of the little girl with the squint.

The rope, which the bell ringer had just let go of, was still quivering at the far end of the church. The sacristan was lighting the last tapers. How many were there in that ghostly gathering of half-asleep people? Fifteen at the most. There were only three men: the sacristan, the bell ringer, and Maigret.

. . . a crime will be committed . . .

At Moulins, the police had treated the matter as a bad joke and had not worried about it. In Paris, they had been surprised to see the chief inspector set off.

Maigret heard some noises behind the door to the right of the altar, and he could guess second by second what was happening: the sacristy, the altar boy arriving late, the priest putting on his chasuble without a word, joining his hands together, and walking toward the nave, followed by the boy, stumbling along in his cassock . . .

The boy was red-haired. He shook his bell. The murmur of the liturgical prayers began.

. . . during the first Mass . . .

Maigret had looked at all the shadowy figures one by one. Five old women, three of

12

whom had a prayer stool reserved for her own use. A farmer's fat wife. Some younger farm women and one child . . .

The sound of a car outside; the creak of the door; some light footsteps: then a lady in mourning walked the whole length of the church.

In the chancel was a row of stalls reserved for people from the chateau, hard seats of polished old wood. And it was there that the woman took her seat, noiselessly, followed by the farm women's eyes.

"Requiem aeternam dona eis, Domine . . ."

Maigret could perhaps still have recited the responses to the priest. He smiled at the thought that in the past he had preferred the Requiem Masses to the others, because the prayers were shorter. He could remember Masses that had been celebrated in sixteen minutes.

But now he had eyes only for the occupant in the Gothic stall. He could barely make out her profile. He hesitated to identify her as Countess de Saint-Fiacre.

"Dies irae, dies illa . . ."

It was she, all right! But when he had last seen her, she was thirty-five or thirty-six. She was a tall, slim, melancholy woman, whom he used to catch sight of from a distance in the park.

Now she would be well into her sixties. She was praying fervently, her emaciated face pale, her long delicate hands clasping a missal.

Maigret had remained in the last row of straw-bottomed chairs, those that cost five centimes at High Mass, but were free at Low Mass.

. . . a crime will be committed . . .

He stood up with the others at the first Gospel. Details attracted his attention on all sides, and memories forced themselves upon him. For example, he suddenly thought:

On All Souls' Day the same priest celebrates three Masses.

In his time, he used to have breakfast at the priest's house between the second and third Masses: a hard-boiled egg and some goat cheese . . .

It was the Moulins police who were right. There couldn't be a crime.

The sacristan had taken his seat at the end of the stalls, four places beyond the countess. The bell ringer had walked away with a heavy tread, like a theatrical producer who has no desire to watch his own production.

There were no other men left but Maigret and the priest, a young priest with the pas-

14

sionate gaze of a mystic. He didn't hurry like the old priest the chief inspector had known. He didn't mumble half the verses.

The stained-glass windows were turning pale. Outside, day was breaking. A cow was lowing on a farm.

And soon everybody was bending double for the Elevation. The altar boy's bell tinkled shrilly.

Maigret was the only one who did not take Communion. All the women walked toward the altar rail, their hands folded, their faces expressionless. Hosts so pale that they seemed unreal passed for a moment through the priest's hands.

The Mass continued. The countess's face was buried in her hands.

"Pater Noster . . ."

"Et ne nos inducas in tentationem . . ."

The old woman's fingers parted, revealed a tormented face, opened the missal.

Another four minutes . . . The prayers, the last Gospel, and then everybody would go out. And there would not have been a crime.

The warning stated clearly: *the first Mass.*

The proof that it was over was that the sacristan was standing up, ready to go into the sacristy.

Countess de Saint-Fiacre's head was buried in her hands once more. She was not moving.

Most of the other women were just as rigid. *"Ite, missa est."* The Mass is over. . . .

Only then did Maigret feel how anxious he had been; he had scarcely realized it as he waited impatiently for the last Gospel. Heaving an involuntary sigh, he was thinking about breathing the fresh air outside, seeing people moving around, hearing them talking about this and that.

The old women woke up all together. Feet shuffled on the cold flagstones of the church. One started for the door, then another. The sacristan appeared with a candle extinguisher, and a thin wisp of blue smoke took the place of each flame.

Day had broken. Gray light was entering the nave along with drafts of air.

Three people were left . . . two. . . . A chair moved. Only the countess remained, and Maigret's nerves became taut with impatience.

The sacristan, who had finished his task, looked at Madame de Saint-Fiacre. A puzzled expression passed across his face. At the same moment, the chief inspector walked forward.

The two of them stood close to her, surprised by her immobility, trying to see the face hidden by the joined hands.

Suddenly alarmed, Maigret touched her

16

shoulder. And the body tipped over, as if it had been balanced on a knife's edge, rolled to the floor, and lay motionless.

Countess de Saint-Fiacre was dead.

The body had been taken into the sacristy, where it had been laid on three chairs placed side by side. The sacristan had run out to get the village doctor.

As a result, Maigret forgot how unusual his presence was. He took several minutes to understand the suspicious inquiry in the priest's burning eyes.

"Who are you?" the man finally asked. "How is it that . . ."

"Chief Inspector Maigret, from the Police Judiciaire."

He looked at the priest. He was a man of about thirty-five, with features that were regular but so solemn that they recalled the fierce faith of monks of old.

The man was profoundly disturbed. A somewhat unsteadier voice murmured:

"You don't mean that . . . ?"

They had not dared undress the countess. They had vainly held a mirror to her lips. They had listened for her heart, which was no longer beating.

"I can't see any wound," was Maigret's only reply.

17

He looked around at this unchangeable scene, in which not a single detail had altered in at least thirty years. The altar cruets were in the same place, the chasuble was prepared for the following Mass, and the altar boy's cassock and surplice were ready.

The dirty light entering through a Gothic window was thinning out the rays of an oil lamp.

It was hot and cold at the same time. The priest was being assailed by terrible thoughts.

Maigret did not see the full drama of the situation at first. But memories from his childhood went on rising to the surface like air bubbles.

A church in which a crime has been committed must be newly consecrated by the bishop. . . .

How could there have been a crime? Nobody had heard a shot. Nobody had approached the countess. During the whole Mass, Maigret had scarcely taken his eyes off her.

And there was no sign of bloodshed, no visible wound.

"The second Mass is at seven o'clock, isn't it?"

It was a relief to hear the heavy footsteps

of the doctor, a red-faced fellow, who was impressed by the atmosphere and looked in turn at the chief inspector and the priest.

"Dead?" he asked.

He did not hesitate to unbutton the countess's blouse, while the priest turned his head away. Heavy steps in the church. Then the bell, which the ringer had set in motion, sounded: the first bell for the seven o'clock Mass.

"I can only suppose that heart failure . . . I wasn't the countess's regular doctor. She preferred to be attended by a colleague in Moulins. But I've been called two or three times to the chateau. . . . She had a very weak heart."

The sacristy was tiny. The three men and the corpse could only just fit inside. Two altar boys arrived, since the seven o'clock was a High Mass.

"Her car must be outside," said Maigret. "We must arrange for her to be taken home."

He could still feel the priest's anguished gaze weighing on him. Had he guessed something? While the sacristan, with the chauffeur's help, was carrying the body to the car, he came over to the chief inspector.

"You're sure that . . . I have another two Masses to say. . . . It's All Souls' Day. My parishioners are . . ."

Since the countess had died of heart failure, wasn't Maigret entitled to reassure the priest?

"You heard what the doctor said."

"All the same, you came here today, to this particular Mass. . . ."

Maigret made an effort not to seem flustered.

"Just a coincidence, Father. . . . My father is buried in your graveyard."

Then he hurried out to the car, a very old one. The chauffeur was cranking the engine, but the doctor did not know what to do. There were a few people in the square, who could not figure out what was happening.

"Come with us."

The corpse took up most of the room inside, but Maigret and the doctor squeezed in.

"You looked surprised at what I told you," murmured the doctor, who had not yet recovered his composure. "If you knew the situation, you might understand. . . . The countess . . ."

He fell silent, glancing at the uniformed chauffeur, who was driving with an absent-minded expression. They crossed the sloping square, which was bordered on one side by the church built on the hillside, and on the other by Nôtre-Dame pond, which, that particular morning, was a poisonous gray color.

Marie Tatin's inn was on the right, the first house in the village. To the left was an avenue of oaks and, in the distance, the dark mass of the chateau.

The sky looked as cold as an ice rink.

"You know this is going to create some complications. . . . That's why the priest looked so upset."

Dr. Bouchardon was a peasant, and the son of peasants. He was wearing a brown shooting outfit and high rubber boots.

"I was off duck shooting by the ponds. . . ."

"You don't go to Mass?"

The doctor winked.

"Mind you, that didn't stop my being on good terms with the old priest. But this one . . ."

They were driving into the park. Now they could make out the details of the chateau: the ground-floor windows, covered by shutters; the two corner towers, the only old parts of the building.

When the car drew up near the steps, Maigret looked down through the latticed ground-level windows and caught a glimpse of steam-filled kitchens and a fat woman plucking partridges.

The chauffeur did not know what to do, and didn't dare open the car doors.

"Monsieur Jean won't be up yet. . . ."

"Call somebody . . . anybody . . . There are some other servants in the house, aren't there?"

Maigret's nostrils were moist. It was really cold. He remained standing in the courtyard with the doctor, who started filling a pipe.

"Who is Monsieur Jean?"

Bouchardon shrugged his shoulders and gave a queer smile.

"You'll see."

"But who is he?"

"A young man . . . A charming young man."

"A relative?"

"If you like . . . In his own way . . . Oh, I might as well tell you right away. He's the countess's lover. Officially, he's her secretary."

Maigret looked at the doctor, remembering that he had been at school with him. But nobody recognized him. He was forty-two. He had put on weight.

As for the chateau, he knew it as well as anybody else, especially the outbuildings. He had to take only a few steps to see the manager's house, where he had been born.

Perhaps it was these memories that were disturbing him so much. Especially the memory of Countess de Saint-Fiacre as he had known her: a young woman who had, for the country boy he had been, personified all that was feminine, graceful, noble.

And now she was dead. They had bundled her like an inanimate object into the car, and they had had to bend her legs. They had not even buttoned up her blouse, and some white underclothing was poking out of her mourning dress.

. . . a crime will be committed . . .

But the doctor maintained that she had died of heart failure. What supernatural power had been able to foretell that? And why call in the police?

People were running about inside the chateau. Doors were opening and shutting. A butler who was only half dressed opened the main door a little, hesitating to come out. A man appeared behind him, in pajamas, his hair tousled, his eyes tired.

"What is it?" he called out.

"The paramour," the cynical doctor growled in Maigret's ear.

The cook had been told too. She was looking silently out of her basement window. Dormer windows were opening at the top of the house, in the servants' rooms.

"Well, why doesn't somebody carry the

23

countess to her room?" Maigret thundered indignantly.

All this struck him as sacrilegious, because it did not tally with his childhood memories. It made him feel not merely morally, but physically, sick.

. . . a crime will be committed . . .

The second bell for Mass was ringing. People must be hurrying. There were farmers who came a long way, in light carts. They had brought flowers to place on the graves.

Jean did not dare to approach. The butler, who had opened the car door, stood there utterly crushed, without moving a muscle.

"Madame the Countess . . . Madame the . . ." he stammered.

"Well? . . . Are you going to leave her there? Eh?"

Why the devil was the doctor smiling so sarcastically?

Maigret used his authority.

"Come on now! Two men . . . You" — he pointed to the chauffeur — "and you" — he pointed to the butler — "carry her up to her room."

While they were reaching into the car, a bell rang in the hall.

"The telephone . . . That's peculiar at this

hour," growled Bouchardon.

Jean did not dare answer it. He seemed to be in a daze. It was Maigret who rushed to pick up the receiver.

"Hello . . . Yes, the chateau . . ."

A voice that seemed very close said:

"Will you ask my mother to come to the telephone? She must be back from Mass by now."

"Who's speaking?"

"Count de Saint-Fiacre . . . But that's none of your business. Let me speak to my mother . . ."

"Just a minute . . . Will you tell me where you're calling from?"

"From Moulins . . . But, I tell you . . ."

"It would be best if you came over here," was all that Maigret said before he hung up.

Then he had to press against the wall to let the body, carried by the two servants, pass by.

— 2 —
The Missal

"Are you coming in?" asked the doctor as soon as the dead woman had been laid on her bed. "I need somebody to help me undress her."

"We'll find a maid," said Maigret.

Jean went up to the next floor and came down a little later with a woman, about thirty, who cast frightened glances around her.

"Go away!" the chief inspector growled at the other servants, who asked for nothing better.

He held Jean back by the sleeve, looked him up and down, and led him into a window recess.

"What terms are you on with the countess's son?"

"But . . . I . . ."

The young man was thin, and his striped pajamas, which were of questionable cleanliness, gave him little presence. His eyes avoided Maigret's. He had a nervous habit of pulling at his fingers as if he wanted to lengthen them.

"Listen," the chief inspector broke in, "we're going to speak plainly, to save time."

Behind the heavy oak door of the bedroom they could hear footsteps coming and going, the creaking of bedsprings, and orders being given in an undertone to the maid by Dr. Bouchardon. The dead woman was being undressed.

"What exactly is your position at the chateau? How long have you been here?"

"Four years . . ."

"How did you come to know Countess de Saint-Fiacre?"

"I . . . that is to say, I was introduced to her by common friends. . . . My parents had just been ruined by the crash of a small bank in Lyons. . . . I came here as confidential secretary, to look after the countess's personal affairs."

"I beg your pardon, but what were you doing before?"

"Traveling. I wrote some art criticism. . . ."

Maigret did not smile. The atmosphere did not lend itself to irony.

The chateau was huge. From the outside it was fairly impressive. But the interior looked as seedy as the young man's pajamas. Dust was everywhere, on old things without any beauty, on a host of useless objects.

The curtains were faded.

And on the walls, paler patches showed that pieces of furniture had been removed. The best pieces, obviously, those that had some value.

"You became the countess's lover?"

"Everybody is free to love whomever . . ."

"Idiot!" growled Maigret, turning his back.

As if things were not obvious. You had only to look at Jean. You had only to breathe the atmosphere of the chateau for a few moments, and catch the servants' glances.

"Did you know that her son was coming?"

"No . . . What does that matter to me?"

His eyes still avoided Maigret's. With his right hand he tugged at the fingers of his left.

"I'd like to get dressed. It's cold. . . . But why are the police bothering about . . . ?"

"Yes, go and get dressed."

Maigret pushed open the bedroom door, and avoided looking toward the bed, on which the dead woman lay completely naked.

The bedroom resembled the rest of the house. It was too big, too cold, cluttered with old bric-à-brac. About to lean on the marble mantelpiece, Maigret noticed that it was broken.

"Have you found anything?" he asked Bouchardon. "Just a moment. Will you please leave us, mademoiselle?"

He closed the door behind the maid, went and pressed his forehead against the window, and let his gaze wander over the park, which was carpeted with leaves and gray mist.

"I can only confirm what I told you earlier. Death was due to sudden heart failure."

"Brought on by . . . ?"

A vague gesture from the doctor, who threw a blanket over the corpse, joined Maigret at the window, and lighted his pipe.

"Perhaps a shock . . . Perhaps the cold . . . Was it cold in the church?"

"Far from it. You didn't find any sign of a wound, of course?"

"No."

"Not even the barely perceptible trace of a prick?"

"I thought of that. . . . No, nothing at all . . . And the countess hasn't imbibed any poison. . . . So you see it would be difficult to maintain . . ."

Maigret was frowning. To the left, under the trees, he could see the red roof of the manager's house, where he had been born.

"In a few words, what is life at the chateau like?" he asked in an undertone.

"You know as much about that as I do. . . . One of those women who are models of good behavior up to the age of forty or forty-five. It was then that the count died, and the son went to Paris to continue his studies."

"And here?"

"Secretaries came, and stayed for longer or shorter periods. You've seen the latest."

"The fortune?"

"The chateau is mortgaged. Three out of every four farms have been sold. Every now and then an antique dealer comes to collect some piece that is still worth something."

"And the son?"

"I can't say I know him very well. They say he's quite a fellow."

"Thank you."

Maigret started to leave the room. Bouchardon followed him.

"Between us, I'd like to know how you happened to be in the church this very morning."

"Yes, it's strange."

"I have a feeling that I've seen you before somewhere."

"That's possible."

And Maigret hurried along the hallway.

His head felt a little empty, because he had not slept long enough. Perhaps he had caught cold, too, at Marie Tatin's inn. He caught sight of Jean going downstairs, dressed in a gray suit but still wearing slippers. At the same moment, a car without a muffler drove into the chateau courtyard.

It was a little sports car, bright yellow, long, narrow, and uncomfortable. A man in a leather coat burst into the hall the next moment, pulling off his cap and shouting:

"Hello! Anybody here? Is everybody still asleep?"

Then he caught sight of Maigret, whom he looked at inquisitively.

"What is it?"

"Shh . . . I must have a word with you."

Near the chief inspector stood Jean, pale, uneasy. As he passed, Count de Saint-Fiacre gave him a gentle punch on the shoulder and said jokingly:

"Still here, you little bastard?"

He did not seem to bear him any malice — just to despise him profoundly.

"There's nothing wrong, is there?"

"Your mother died this morning, in church."

Maurice de Saint-Fiacre was thirty years old, the same age as Jean. They were the same

31

height, but the count was broad-shouldered and a little heavy. Everything about him, especially his cap and leather coat, breathed life and gaiety. His bright eyes were cheerful and mocking.

It needed Maigret's words to make him frown.

"What did you say?"

"Come this way."

"Well, I'll be damned. . . . And I was . . ."

"You were . . . ?"

"Nothing . . . Where is she?"

He was dazed, dumbfounded. In the bedroom, he raised the blanket just enough to see the dead woman's face. There was no explosion of grief. No tears. No dramatic gestures. Just three murmured words.

"Poor old girl!"

Jean had come as far as the door, and the other, catching sight of him, snapped at him:

"Get out!"

He was becoming agitated. He paced up and down the room and bumped into the doctor.

"What did she die of, Bouchardon?"

"Heart failure, Monsieur Maurice . . . But the chief inspector may know more about that than I do."

The young man swung around to face Maigret.

"You're from the police? . . . What . . . ?"

"Could we have a few minutes' conversation? . . . I'd like to take a little walk up the road. . . . You're staying here, aren't you, Doctor?"

"The fact is, I was going shooting."

"Well, you can go shooting another day."

Maurice de Saint-Fiacre accompanied Maigret, gazing thoughtfully at the ground in front of him. When they reached the main drive of the chateau, the seven o'clock Mass had just finished, and the parishioners, more of them than at the first Mass, were coming out and forming groups in the square. A few people were going into the graveyard; only their heads showed above the wall.

As the sky grew lighter, the cold became sharper, probably on account of the north wind, which was sweeping the dead leaves from one side of the square to the other, making them spin around like birds over Nôtre-Dame pond.

Maigret filled his pipe. Wasn't that his chief reason for taking his companion outside? Yet the doctor had smoked even in the dead woman's room, and Maigret was in the habit of smoking anywhere.

But not in the chateau! That was a place apart, which throughout his youth had represented all that was most inaccessible.

"Today the count called me into his library

33

to work with him," his father used to say, with a hint of pride in his voice.

And the boy that Maigret had been at that time used to gaze respectfully, from a distance, at the baby carriage being pushed around the park by a nursemaid. The baby in it was Maurice de Saint-Fiacre.

"Does anybody stand to benefit from your mother's death?"

"I don't understand. The doctor just said . . ."

He was uneasy. His gestures were jerky. He snatched the piece of paper Maigret held out to him, the one that foretold the crime.

"What does this mean? Bouchardon spoke of heart failure, and . . ."

"Heart failure that somebody foresaw a fortnight in advance!"

Some farmers were looking at them from a distance. The two men approached the church, walking slowly, following the train of their thoughts.

"What were you coming to the chateau for this morning?"

"That's exactly what I was thinking," said the young man. "You asked me just now . . . Well, yes, there *is* somebody who stands to benefit from my mother's death. . . . Me!"

He was not joking. His forehead was furrowed. He greeted by name a man going by on a bicycle.

"Since you're from the police, you must understand the situation already. . . . Besides, that fellow Bouchardon is sure to have talked. . . . My mother was a poor girl. My father died. I went away. Left by herself, I can well believe, her mind might have become slightly unhinged. . . . First of all, she spent most of her time at church. Then . . ."

"The young secretaries . . . ?"

"I don't think it was what you think, and what Bouchardon would like to suggest. Nothing immoral . . . Just a longing for affection, the urge to look after somebody . . . The fact that those young men took advantage of that to go further . . . Mind you, that didn't prevent her from remaining very pious. She must have had some terrible attacks of conscience, torn as she was between her faith and that . . . that . . ."

"You were saying that you stand to benefit?"

"You know that there isn't very much of our fortune left. And people like that young man you've seen have hearty appetites. . . . Let's say that in another three or four years there'd have been nothing left at all."

He was bareheaded. He ran his fingers through his hair. Then, looking straight at

Maigret, he added, after a pause:

"The only thing left for me to tell you is that I was coming here today to ask my mother for forty thousand francs. I need those forty thousand francs to cover a check that will otherwise bounce. . . . You see how everything ties up."

He broke a twig off a hedge they were passing. He seemed to be making a violent effort to prevent himself from being overwhelmed by what had happened.

"And to think that I've brought Marie Vassilief with me!"

"Marie Vassilief?"

"My mistress . . . I've left her in bed in Moulins. . . . She's quite capable of hiring a car and driving over here. . . . That would top everything, wouldn't it?"

They were just putting out the lamp in Marie Tatin's inn, where a few men were drinking rum. The bus from Moulins was about to leave, half empty.

"She didn't deserve it!" said the count, in a thoughtful voice.

"Who?"

"Mother."

At that moment there was something childlike about him, in spite of his height and slight paunchiness. Perhaps he was at last on the verge of tears.

The two men walked up and down near the church, covering the same ground over and over again, sometimes facing the pond, sometimes with their backs to it.

"Look, Chief Inspector . . . Nobody could have killed her. . . . Or else I don't understand."

Maigret thought about that, and so hard that he forgot about his companion. He was recalling every little detail of the first Mass:

The countess in her pew . . . Nobody had gone near her. She had taken Communion. Next she had knelt down with her face in her hands. Then she had opened her missal. A little later, her face was in her hands again. . . .

"Excuse me for a moment . . ."

Maigret went up the steps and entered the church, where the sacristan was preparing the altar again. The bell ringer, a rough peasant wearing heavy hobnailed boots, was straightening the chairs.

The chief inspector walked straight up to the stalls, bent down, then called the sacristan.

"Who picked up the missal?"

"What missal?"

"The countess's . . . It was left here."

"You think so?"

"Come here," Maigret said to the bell ringer. "You haven't seen the missal that was in this seat, have you?"

"Me?"

Either he was an idiot or he was pretending to be. Maigret was on edge. He caught sight of Maurice de Saint-Fiacre standing at the far end of the nave.

"Who has been near this stall?"

"The doctor's wife sat here at the seven o'clock Mass."

"I thought the doctor wasn't a believer?"

"He may not be. But his wife . . ."

"Well, you tell the whole village that there'll be a big reward for whoever brings me the missal."

"At the chateau?"

"No. At Marie Tatin's."

Outside, Maurice de Saint-Fiacre fell in beside him again.

"I can't make head or tail of this missal business."

"Heart failure, wasn't it? That may have been brought on by a severe shock. And it happened shortly after Communion. In other words, after the countess opened her missal . . . Suppose that in that missal . . ."

But the young man shook his head, looking discouraged.

"I can't imagine any piece of news capable of shocking my mother to that extent. . . . Besides, it would be . . . so horrible."

He was breathing hard. He stared gloomily at the chateau.

"Let's go and have a drink."

He did not head for the chateau, but for the inn, where his entry created a certain embarrassment. The four farmers drinking there suddenly felt no longer at home. They greeted the count with a respect mingled with fear.

Marie Tatin ran out of the kitchen, wiping her hands on her apron. She stammered:

"Monsieur Maurice . . . I'm still upset by the news. . . . Our poor countess . . ."

She at least was crying. She probably wept buckets every time anybody died in the village.

"You were at the Mass too, weren't you?" she said, calling Maigret to witness. "When I think that none of us noticed anything! It was here that I heard . . ."

It is always disconcerting in such circumstances to show less grief than do people who ought to be indifferent. The count listened to these expressions of sympathy, trying to hide his impatience, and, to keep it from showing, he took a bottle of rum from the shelf and filled a couple of glasses. His shoulders were shaken by a shudder as he drained his glass in one gulp. He said to Maigret:

"I think I caught cold coming here this morning."

"Everybody here has a cold, Monsieur Maurice," Marie Tatin said.

And, to Maigret:

"You ought to take care too. I heard you coughing last night. . . . "

The farmers left. The stove was red hot.

"A day like today!" said Marie Tatin.

Because of her squint, it was impossible to say whether she was looking at Maigret or the count.

"Won't you have something to eat? I was so upset when I heard . . . that I didn't even think of changing my dress."

She had simply tied an apron over the black dress she put on only to go to Mass. Her hat had been left on a table.

Maurice de Saint-Fiacre drank a second glass of rum, and looked at Maigret as if to ask him what to do.

"Come along!" said the chief inspector.

"Don't you want to have lunch here? I've killed a chicken and . . ."

But the two men were already outside. In front of the church were four or five carts; the horses were tied to trees. Heads could be seen moving beyond the low wall of the

40

graveyard. The yellow car in the courtyard of the chateau was the only patch of bright color.

"Has the check been cashed?" asked Maigret.

"It *will* be tomorrow."

"Do you do much work?"

A pause. There was the sound of their footsteps on the frozen road, the rustle of dead leaves carried along by the wind, horses snorting.

"I'm exactly what people mean by a good-for-nothing. I've done a little of everything. . . . Look, the forty thousand . . . I wanted to start a film company. Before that, I was a partner in a broadcasting business."

A dull explosion sounded on the right, beyond Nôtre-Dame pond. They caught sight of a hunter striding toward the animal he had killed, which his dog was worrying at.

"That's Gautier, the estate manager," said the count. "He must have gone out shooting before . . ."

Then all of a sudden he lost his self-control, stamped his foot, made a face, and nearly let out a sob.

"Poor old girl!" he muttered, drawing back his lips. "It's . . . it's so disgusting. . . . And that little bastard Jean, who . . ."

As if by magic, they suddenly saw the fellow pacing up and down the courtyard of the chateau with the doctor, obviously talking excitedly, since he was gesticulating with his thin arms.

In the wind, every now and then, they could catch the scent of chrysanthemums.

— 3 —

The Altar Boy

There was no sunshine to mar the picture, no mist, either, to blur the contours. Everything stood out with cruel clarity: the tree trunks, the dead branches, the gravel, and, above all, the black clothes of the people who had come to the graveyard. The whites, on the other hand — tombstones, starched shirt fronts, old women's bonnets — took on an unreal, deceptive tone: whites that were too white and seemed out of place.

Without the dry north wind, which cut your cheeks, you might have thought you were under a rather dusty glass cloche.

"I'll see you again later."

Maigret left Count de Saint-Fiacre outside the gate of the graveyard. An old woman, sitting on a little stool she had brought with her, was trying to sell oranges and chocolate.

The oranges were big and ripe and frozen. They set the teeth on edge and rasped the throat, but, when he was ten years old, Maigret used to eat them greedily all the same, because they were oranges.

He turned up the velvet collar of his coat. He did not look at anybody. He knew that he had to turn left, and that the grave he was looking for was the third after the cypresses.

All around, flowers had been placed on graves. The day before, women had washed some of the tombstones with soap and water. The railings had been repainted.

HERE LIES EVARISTE MAIGRET

"Excuse me! No smoking . . ."

The chief inspector scarcely realized that he was being spoken to. Finally he stared at the bell ringer, who was also the graveyard keeper, and thrust his lighted pipe into his pocket.

He could not manage to think about one thing at a time. Memories flooded in on him, memories of his father, of a friend who had drowned in Nôtre-Dame pond, and of the child at the chateau in his handsome baby carriage . . .

People looked at him. He looked at them. He had already seen those faces. But before, that man who had a child in his arms, for example, and was accompanied by a pregnant woman, had been a boy of four or five. . . .

Maigret had no flowers. The tombstone

was dirty. He walked out of the graveyard in a bad mood, making a whole group turn around as he muttered:

"The first thing we must do is find the missal!"

He did not feel like returning to the chateau. Something there distressed him, made him indignant even.

Admittedly, he had no illusions about humanity. But he was furious that his childhood memories had been sullied. The countess, above all, whom he had always seen as a noble, beautiful person, like a picture-book heroine.

Now she turned out to be a crazy old woman who kept a succession of gigolos.

And not even that. It wasn't frank and open. The notorious Jean pretended to be her secretary. He was not handsome, and not very young either.

And the poor old woman, as her son said, was torn between the chateau and the church.

And the last Count de Saint-Fiacre was going to be arrested for passing a bad check.

Somebody was walking in front of Maigret with a gun on his shoulder, and the chief inspector suddenly realized that he was moving toward the estate manager's house. He thought he could recognize the figure

45

he had seen from a distance, in the fields.

A few feet separated the two men when they reached the yard, where some hens were nestling against a wall, sheltering from the wind, their feathers quivering.

"Hey!"

The man with the gun turned around.

"You're the Saint-Fiacres' manager, aren't you?"

"And who are you?"

"Chief Inspector Maigret, from the Police Judiciaire."

"Maigret?"

The manager was struck by the name, but could not place it.

"You've heard the news?"

"I've just been told. I was out shooting. . . . What are the police . . . ?"

He was a short, sturdy, gray-haired man with skin furrowed by fine, deep wrinkles, and eyes that looked as if they were lying in ambush behind thick brows.

"They told me that her heart . . ."

"Where are you going?"

"Well, I can't go into the chateau with my boots caked with mud and my gun. . . ."

A rabbit's head was hanging from the game bag. Maigret looked at the house toward which they were walking.

"Well, well! They've changed the kitchen."

A suspicious gaze was fixed on him.

"A good fifteen years ago," growled the manager.

"What's your name?"

"Gautier . . . Is it true that the count arrived without . . ."

All this was hesitant, reticent. And when Gautier pushed open the door, he did not ask Maigret to come in.

The chief inspector walked in just the same, and turned right toward the dining room, which smelled of biscuits and old brandy.

"Come in here for a moment, Monsieur Gautier. They don't need you over there. And I have a few questions to ask you. . . ."

"Hurry up!" said a woman's voice in the kitchen. "They say it's awful. . . ."

Maigret felt the oak table, which had corners decorated with carved lions. It was the same table as in his time. It had been sold to the new manager when his father died.

"You'll have something to drink?"

Gautier took a bottle out of the sideboard, perhaps to save time.

"What do you think of that Monsieur Jean? . . . Now I come to think of it, what's his surname?"

"Métayer . . . Quite a good Bourges family . . ."

"Did he cost the countess a lot?"

47

Gautier filled glasses with brandy but remained stubbornly silent.

"What does he have to do at the chateau? As manager, you probably look after everything."

"Everything!"

"Well?"

"He doesn't do anything. . . . A few personal letters . . . In the beginning, he claimed to be able to make money for the countess, thanks to his financial knowledge. He bought some shares, which dropped in value in a few months. . . . He maintained that he'd get everything back thanks to a new photographic process one of his friends had invented. That cost the countess about a hundred thousand francs, and the friend disappeared. . . . The latest thing was some business of printing with negatives. . . . I don't know anything about it. Something like photogravure, but cheaper . . ."

"Jean Métayer was very busy, in fact . . . ?"

"He bustled around a lot for nothing. . . . He wrote some articles for the *Journal de Moulins,* and they were forced to accept them because of the countess. It was there that he tried out his negatives, and the editor didn't dare throw him out. . . . Good health!"

Suddenly anxious, he asked:

"Nothing's happened between him and the count?"

"Nothing at all."

"I suppose it's just a coincidence, your being here. . . . There's no reason you should be, seeing it was a case of heart disease. . . ."

The trouble was that it was impossible to meet the manager's eyes. He wiped his mustache and moved toward the next room.

"Will you excuse me while I change? I was going to go to Mass, and now . . ."

"I'll see you later," said Maigret as he left.

He had no sooner shut the door than he heard the woman, who had remained invisible, ask:

"Who was that?"

They had laid paving stones in the yard where he used to play marbles on packed earth.

The square was full of groups of people in their Sunday best, and organ music was coming from the church. The children, in their best clothes, did not dare play. And everywhere handkerchiefs were being brought out of pockets, red noses being blown noisily.

Snatches of conversation reached Maigret's ears:

"He's a policeman from Paris. . . ."

"They say he's come about the cow that died last week at Mathieu's. . . ."

A young man dressed up in a navy-blue suit with a red flower in his buttonhole, his face well scrubbed, his hair shining with brilliantine, ventured to say to the chief inspector:

"They're waiting for you at Tatin's about the boy who stole . . ."

And he nudged his companions, holding back a laugh, which burst out when he turned his head away.

He was telling the truth. At Marie Tatin's, the atmosphere was now warmer and thicker. Pipes and pipes of tobacco had been smoked. A family of peasants at one table was eating food they had brought from the farm and drinking large bowls of coffee. The father was cutting a dried sausage with his pocket-knife.

The young men were drinking lemonade, and the old men brandy. Marie Tatin was kept trotting around without cease.

In one corner, a woman stood up when the chief inspector came in and took a step toward him, worried, hesitant, moist-lipped. She had one hand on the shoulder of a small boy, whose red hair Maigret recognized.

"Are you the chief inspector?"

Everybody looked in her direction.

"First of all, Chief Inspector, I want to tell you our family has always been honest . . . even though we're poor. You understand? . . . When I saw that Ernest . . ."

The boy, very pale, stared straight ahead without showing the slightest emotion.

"Was it you who took the missal?" asked Maigret, bending down.

No reply. A wild, piercing look.

"Answer the chief inspector."

But the boy did not open his mouth. In a flash, the mother gave him a slap that left a red mark on his left cheek. The boy's head shook for a moment, his eyes became somewhat moist, his lips trembled, but he did not budge.

"Are you going to answer, curse of my life?"

And to Maigret she said:

"There's today's children for you! . . . He's been crying for months to get me to buy him a missal. A thick one, like the curé's! Have you ever heard the like? . . . So when I heard about Madame the Countess's missal, I thought right away. . . Besides, I was surprised to see him come home between the second Mass and the third. Usually he eats at the rectory. . . . I went up to his room and I found this under the mattress."

Once again the mother's hand descended on the boy's cheek. He made no attempt to ward off the blow.

"When I was his age, I couldn't even read. But I'd never have had enough wickedness in me to steal a book."

There was a respectful silence in the inn. Maigret had the missal in his hands.

"Thank you, madame."

He was in a hurry to examine it and started to walk to the far end of the room.

"Chief Inspector . . ."

The woman, calling him back, looked embarrassed.

"They told me there was a reward. . . . It isn't because Ernest . . ."

Maigret handed her twenty francs, which she put carefully away in her bag. Then she pulled her son toward the door, grumbling:

"As for you, you thief, you just wait!"

Maigret's eyes met the boy's. It was a matter of only a few seconds. Still, they both understood that they were friends.

Perhaps it was because Maigret, in his childhood, had longed for — and never possessed — a gilt-edged missal with, not only the Ordinary of the Mass, but also all the liturgical texts, in two columns, in Latin and French.

"What time will you be coming back to eat?"

"I don't know."

Maigret nearly went up to his room to examine the missal, but the memory of the countless drafts the roof let in made him choose the main road.

It was while walking slowly toward the chateau that he opened the book, whose binding was embossed with the Saint-Fiacre coat of arms. Actually, he did not open it; the missal opened itself at a page where a piece of paper had been inserted.

Page 221. Prayers after Communion.

What was there was a piece of newspaper cut out jaggedly, which immediately struck the eye as most peculiar, because it had been so badly printed.

PARIS, *1 November. A dramatic suicide took place this morning in a flat on Rue de Miromesnil that had been occupied for several years by Count de Saint-Fiacre and his mistress, a Russian woman named Marie V . . .*

After telling his mistress that he was ashamed of the scandalous conduct of a certain member of his family, the count fired a bullet into his head and died a few

*minutes later without recovering conscious-
ness.*

*We understand that a distressing family
drama lies behind this incident and that
the person mentioned above is none other
than the dead man's mother.*

A goose wandering onto the road stretched
out toward Maigret a beak wide open in
fury. The bell was in full peal, and the con-
gregation was shuffling slowly out of the
little church, from which the odors of incense
and extinguished tapers were escaping.

Maigret had thrust the bulky missal into
his coat pocket, where it made a bulge, when
he stopped to examine the fateful scrap of
paper.

The murder weapon! A newspaper clipping two inches by three!

Countess de Saint-Fiacre went to the first
Mass and knelt down in the stall that for
two centuries had been reserved for mem-
bers of her family.

And here was the weapon that killed her.
Maigret turned the piece of paper over and
over. It was really peculiar. Among other
things, he noticed the alignment of the type,
and felt sure that the printing had not been
done on a rotary press, used for a real newspaper.

This was just a proof, pulled by hand. That was obvious from the fact that the other side of the paper bore exactly the same text.

The murderer had not taken the trouble to produce a finished piece of work, or else had not had enough time. Besides, would the countess be likely to think of turning the piece of paper over? Wouldn't she have died first from shock, indignation, shame, and fear?

The expression on Maigret's face was terrible, because he had never before encountered a crime so cowardly and so clever at the same time.

And the murderer had had the nerve to warn the police!

Suppose the missal had not been found . . .

Yes, that was it! The missal was not intended to be found! Without it, it would be impossible to talk about a crime, or to accuse anybody. The countess had died from heart failure.

He turned around suddenly, and arrived at Marie Tatin's to find everybody talking about him and the missal.

"You know where little Ernest lives?"

"Third house after the grocer's, on the High Street . . ."

He hurried there. It was a small single-story house. There were photographs of the father and mother above the sideboard. The woman, who had already changed out of her Sunday best, was in the kitchen, which smelled of roast beef.

"Is your son here?"

"He's changing. There's no point in getting his best clothes dirty. You saw what a scolding I gave him! A child who has nothing but good examples in front of him and . . ."

She opened the door and shouted:

"Come here, you bad boy!"

He caught sight of the boy in his underpants, trying to hide.

"Let him get dressed," said Maigret. "I'll talk to him then."

The woman went on preparing the dinner. Her husband was presumably at Marie Tatin's having his apéritif.

At last the door opened, and Ernest came in, with a sly look on his face, wearing his weekday suit, the trousers of which were too long.

"You want him to go out with you?" exclaimed the woman. "But in that case . . . Ernest, go and put your best suit on, quick!"

"It isn't worth it, madame. Come along, boy."

The street was empty. All the life of the district was concentrated in the square, in the graveyard, and at Marie Tatin's.

"Tomorrow I'm going to give you an even thicker missal, with the first letter of every word in red."

The boy was dumbfounded. So the chief inspector knew that there were missals with red letters, like the one on the altar.

"But you're going to tell me honestly where you found this one. I won't scold you."

It was strange to see the old peasant mistrust awakening in the boy. He said nothing. He was already on the defensive.

"Was it on the prayer stool that you found it?"

Silence. There were freckles on his cheeks and the bridge of his nose. His thick lips were trying to keep still.

"Don't you understand that I'm your friend?"

"Yes . . . You gave Ma twenty francs."

"Well, what of it?"

The child took his revenge.

"When we got back home, Ma told me she'd only slapped me for show, and she gave me fifty centimes."

The boy knew what he was doing, all right. What was going on inside that head of his, which was too big for his thin body?

"And what about the sacristan?"

"He didn't say anything to me."

"Who took the missal from the prayer stool?"

"I don't know."

"Where did you find it?"

"Under my surplice, in the sacristy . . . I was supposed to go and have breakfast in the rectory, but I'd forgotten my handkerchief. When I moved my surplice, I felt something hard."

"Was the sacristan there?"

"He was in the church, putting out the candles. . . . You know, a missal with red letters costs an awful lot."

In other words, somebody had taken the missal from the prayer stool and had hidden it for the time being in the sacristy, under the altar boy's surplice, obviously with the intention of coming back for it later.

"Did you open it?"

"I didn't have time. . . . I wanted my boiled egg. Because on Sunday . . ."

"I know."

And Ernest wondered how this man from Paris could possibly know that on Sunday he had an egg and some bread and jam at the rectory.

"You can go."

"Is it true that I'll have . . . ?"

"A missal, yes . . . Tomorrow. Good-bye."

Maigret held out his hand, and after a

moment's hesitation the boy gave him his.

"I know you're just joking," he said, however, as he went off.

A crime in three stages: somebody had set the article, or had it set, on a linotype, which could be found only in a newspaper office or a big printing plant.

Somebody had slipped the piece of paper into the missal, after choosing the page.

And somebody had collected the missal and hidden it temporarily under the surplice in the sacristy.

Perhaps the same man had done everything. Perhaps each operation had been carried out by a different person. Or perhaps the same person had been responsible for two of the three operations.

As he was passing in front of the church, Maigret saw the priest come out and walk toward him. He waited for him under the poplars, near the woman selling oranges and chocolate.

"I'm going to the chateau," he said as he joined the chief inspector. "That's the first time I've celebrated Mass without knowing what I was doing. The idea that a crime . . ."

"It was a crime, all right," said Maigret laconically.

They walked along in silence. Without saying a word, the chief inspector held out the scrap of paper to his companion, who read it and handed it back.

They walked another hundred yards without speaking.

"One evil leads to another. . . . But she was a poor creature."

They had to hold on to their hats because the wind was increasing in violence.

"I wasn't strict enough," the priest added in a gloomy voice.

"You?"

"Every day she would come back to me. She was ready to return to the ways of the Lord. . . . But every day, over there . . ."

There was a bitter note in his voice.

"I refused to go there, and yet it was my duty."

They nearly stopped, because two men were walking along the main drive of the chateau and they were bound to meet them. They recognized the doctor, with his little brown beard, and, beside him, the tall, thin figure of Jean Métayer, still talking excitedly. The yellow car was in the courtyard. Maigret guessed that Métayer did not dare go back to the chateau as long as Count de Saint-Fiacre was there.

There was an ambiguous light over the village. The situation was ambiguous too, with all these vague comings and goings.

"Come along!" said Maigret.

The doctor must have said the same thing to the secretary, who tagged behind him. When he was near enough he said:

"Good morning, Father. You know, I'm in a position to reassure you. Sinner though I am, I can imagine your distress at the idea that a crime may have been committed in your church. Well, no . . . Science is categorical. *Our* countess died from heart failure."

Maigret had gone up to Métayer.

"I'd like to ask you a question."

He could sense that the young man was on edge, almost panting with fear.

"When did you last go to the *Journal de Moulins*?"

"I . . . Wait a minute . . ."

He was about to answer, but his suspicions were aroused. He darted a distrustful look at the chief inspector.

"Why do you ask that?"

"It doesn't matter why."

"Am I obliged to reply?"

"You are free to say nothing."

Perhaps not exactly the face of a degenerate, but it was an anxious, tormented face. And quite exceptional nervousness, capable of interesting Dr. Bouchardon, who was still talking to the priest.

"I know that I'm the one who's going to suffer! But I'm not going to take it lying down. . . ."

"Of course you're not going to take it lying down. . . ."

"First, I want to see a lawyer. I'm entitled to that. . . . Besides, by what right are you . . . ?"

"Just a minute! Have you ever studied law?"

"For two years."

He was trying to regain his composure, to smile.

"Nobody has made a charge, and nobody has been caught in flagrante delicto. So you've no right to . . ."

"Very good! Ten out of ten!"

"The doctor says . . ."

"And I maintain that the countess was killed by the dirtiest swine imaginable. Read this!"

Maigret held the printed piece of paper out to him. Stiffening suddenly, Métayer looked at him as if he was going to spit in his face.

"You said . . . ? I won't stand for . . ."

The chief inspector, gently putting his hand on his shoulder, said:

"But, my poor young man, I haven't said anything yet, *to you*. Where's the count?

. . . Read that, even so. You can give it back to me later."

A gleam of triumph shone in Métayer's eyes.

"The count is discussing money with the manager. You'll find them in the library."

The priest and the doctor were walking in front, and Maigret heard the doctor say:

"Certainly not, Father. It's human! Terribly human! If only you'd studied a little physiology instead of poring over the writings of Saint Augustine."

The gravel crunched under the feet of the four men, who soon began slowly climbing the steps, which the cold had made whiter and harder than usual.

— 4 —

Marie Vassilief

Maigret could not be everywhere. The chateau was huge. That was why he had only a vague idea of the morning's events.

It was the time when, on Sundays and holidays, the peasants put off the moment of going home, savoring the pleasure of being in a well-dressed group in the village square or in a café. Some were now drunk. Others were talking in loud voices. And the children, in their best clothes, were looking admiringly at their fathers.

In the chateau, Jean Métayer, looking rather yellow, had gone upstairs alone. He could be heard walking up and down.

"If you'll come with me," the doctor said to the priest, luring him in the direction of the dead woman's bedroom.

On the ground floor, a wide hallway ran the entire length of the building, lined by doors. Maigret could hear a hum of voices. He had been told that Count de Saint-Fiacre and the manager were in the library.

He decided to go there, opened the wrong

door, and found himself in a drawing room. The door leading from it to the library was open. In a gilt-edged mirror he caught sight of the reflection of the young man, sitting on a corner of a desk, looking utterly depressed, and the manager solidly planted on his stocky legs.

"You ought to have known there was no point in insisting," Gautier was saying. "Especially for forty thousand francs!"

"Who answered the telephone when I called?"

"Monsieur Jean, of course."

"So he didn't even pass the message on to my mother?"

Maigret coughed and walked into the library.

"What telephone call are you talking about?"

Maurice de Saint-Fiacre answered, without any embarrassment:

"The one I made the day before yesterday to the chateau. As I've already told you, I needed some money. I wanted to ask my mother for it. But it was that . . . that Monsieur Jean, as they call him here, who answered the telephone."

"And he told you there was no chance? Yet you came here all the same. . . ."

The manager was watching the two men.

The count had left the desk on which he had been perched and faced Maigret.

"Anyway, I didn't bring Gautier here to talk about that," he said irritably. "I haven't concealed the situation from you, Chief Inspector. Tomorrow a charge will be laid against me. It's obvious that, with my mother dead, I'm the only natural heir. I therefore asked Gautier to get me forty thousand francs for tomorrow morning. Well, it seems that's impossible."

"Quite impossible!" repeated the manager.

"Apparently nothing can be done without the permission of the lawyer, who won't gather the interested parties together until after the funeral. And, quite apart from that, Gautier says it would be difficult to raise forty thousand francs on the property that remains."

He started walking up and down.

"It's clear, isn't it? All cut and dried! I may even be prevented from attending the funeral. . . . But now I think of it, one more question. You spoke of a crime. . . . Is it . . . ?"

"No charge has been laid, and probably no charge will be laid," said Maigret. "So no case will come before the courts."

"Leave us alone, Gautier."

As soon as the manager had reluctantly left the room, he went on:

"A crime, really?"

"A crime that doesn't concern the police."

"Explain yourself . . . I'm beginning to . . ."

But just then they heard a woman's voice in the hall, accompanied by the deeper voice of the manager. The count frowned and made for the door, which he pulled open abruptly.

"Marie! What the . . . ?"

"Maurice! Why won't they let me in? . . . It's insufferable! I've been waiting for hours at the hotel."

She spoke with a pronounced foreign accent. It was Marie Vassilief, who had arrived from Moulins in an old taxi, which they could see in the courtyard.

She was tall and very beautiful, with hair perhaps artificially fair. Noticing that Maigret was looking at her closely, she started talking volubly in English, and the count answered her in the same language.

She asked him if he had any money. He replied that there was no longer any question of that, that his mother was dead, and that she must go back to Paris, where he would join her soon.

At this she asked, with a laugh:

"What shall I use for money? I haven't even enough to pay for the taxi!"

Maurice de Saint-Fiacre began to panic. His mistress's shrill voice rang through the chateau, giving a scandalous quality to the scene.

The manager was still standing there in the hallway.

"If you stay here, I'm staying with you," declared Marie Vassilief.

Maigret told Gautier:

"Pay the driver and send him away."

The confusion was growing. Not a material, reparable confusion, but a moral confusion, which seemed to be contagious. Gautier, too, was losing his composure.

"I must have a word with you, Chief Inspector," the young man said.

"Not now."

He gestured toward the aggressively elegant woman, who was walking around the library and drawing room as if she were compiling an inventory.

"Who is this silly portrait of, Maurice?" she exclaimed with a laugh.

There were footsteps on the stairs. Maigret saw Métayer go past, wearing a loose coat and carrying a bag. Métayer must have guessed he would not be allowed to leave, because he stopped outside the library door and waited.

"Where are *you* going?"

"To the inn . . . It's more fitting that I should . . ."

To get rid of his mistress, Maurice de Saint-Fiacre took her off toward the right wing of the chateau. The two continued talking in English.

"Is it true that it would be impossible to raise a loan of forty thousand francs on the chateau?" Maigret asked the manager.

"It would be difficult."

"Well, do it anyway, by tomorrow morning at the latest."

The chief inspector was reluctant to leave. After hesitating, he decided to go upstairs. There, a surprise was waiting for him. While downstairs everybody was bustling about aimlessly, order had been restored in Countess de Saint-Fiacre's bedroom.

It no longer had the ambiguous, sordid atmosphere of that morning. It was no longer even the same body. The dead woman, clothed in a white nightdress, was stretched out on her fourposter in a peaceful, dignified attitude, her hands folded on a crucifix.

There were lighted tapers, holy water, and a sprig of boxwood in a bowl.

Bouchardon looked at Maigret as he came in and seemed to be saying:

"Well, what do you think? Nice work, isn't it?"

The priest was praying, moving his lips silently. He remained alone with the dead woman when the other two left.

The groups in the square had thinned out. Through the curtains in the windows of nearby houses, families could be seen sitting at their meal.

For a few seconds, the sun tried to penetrate the layer of clouds, but the next moment the sky turned gray again and the trees trembled more than before.

Jean Métayer, at the inn, was installed in the corner near the window and was eating automatically, looking at the empty road. Maigret had taken a seat at the other end of the room. Between the two of them was a family from a neighboring village who had arrived in a truck. They had brought their own food, and Marie Tatin was serving them drinks.

The poor woman was upset. She could no longer make head or tail of what was happening. Usually she rented an attic room only from time to time, to a workman who came to carry out repairs at the chateau or on a farm.

And now, besides Maigret, she had a new guest: the countess's secretary.

She did not dare ask questions. All morning she had heard frightening stories, told by her customers. Among other things, she had heard mention of the police.

"I'm very much afraid the chicken is over-cooked," she said as she served Maigret.

Her tone of voice was the same in which she would have said:

"I'm afraid of everything! I don't know what's happening! Mother of God, protect me!"

The chief inspector gazed at her tenderly. She had always had this same timid, sickly look.

"Do you remember, Marie, the . . ."

She opened her eyes wide and moved as though to protect herself.

". . . business of the frogs?"

"But . . . Who . . . ?"

"Your mother sent you to pick mushrooms in the meadow beyond Nôtre-Dame pond. There were three small boys playing there. They took advantage of a moment when you were thinking of something else and re-placed the mushrooms in the basket with frogs. And all the way home you were fright-ened because things were moving . . ."

She had been looking at him closely and now stammered:

"Maigret?"

"Shh! Monsieur Jean has finished his chicken and is waiting for the next course."

Marie Tatin changed. She was more agitated than before, but seemed to have moments of confidence.

How funny life was! Years and years without the slightest incident, without anything happening to relieve the daily monotony. And then, all of a sudden, incomprehensible events, dramatic happenings, things such as you did not even read about in the papers!

Now and then, while waiting on Jean Métayer and the farmers, she darted a conspiratorial glance at Maigret. When he had finished his meal, she said shyly:

"You'll have a glass of brandy, won't you?"

"You used to say *tu* in the old days, Marie!"

She laughed. No, she did not dare to any more.

"But *you* haven't had any lunch!"

"Yes, I have! I never stop eating in the kitchen. A mouthful now . . . a mouthful later . . ."

A motorcycle went by. Maigret caught a glimpse of a young man who looked better dressed than most of the inhabitants of Saint-Fiacre.

"Who's that?"

"Didn't you see him this morning? It's Emile Gautier, the manager's son."

"Where is he going?"

"Probably to Moulins . . . He's practically

a city boy. He works in a bank."

People could be seen coming out of their houses, walking along the road, or making for the graveyard.

Curiously, Maigret was sleepy. He felt harassed, as if he had made an exceptional effort. And this was not because he had got up at half past five in the morning, nor because he had caught a cold.

It was the atmosphere that was crushing him. He felt personally affected by the drama, disgusted by it.

Yes, disgusted. That was the word for it. He had never imagined that he would find his native village in such circumstances. Down to his father's grave, the tombstone turned black; and he had been forbidden to smoke! Facing him at the other end of the room, Jean Métayer knew he was being watched and was trying to keep calm and even to put on a vaguely contemptuous smile.

"A glass of brandy?" Marie Tatin asked him too.

"No, thank you. I never touch alcohol."

He was well-bred. He made a point of displaying his good manners at every opportunity. At the inn, he ate with the same affected gestures he had used at the chateau.

When he finished eating, he asked:

"Have you a telephone?"

"No, but there's one over there."

He crossed the road and went into the grocer's shop, run by the sacristan, where a telephone was installed. He must have asked for long distance, because Maigret saw him waiting a long time in the shop, smoking one cigarette after another.

When he returned, the farmers had left the inn. Marie Tatin was washing glasses in readiness for Vespers, which would bring more customers.

"Who did you just telephone? Remember that I can find out by asking the operator."

"My father, in Bourges."

His voice was curt, aggressive.

"I asked him to send me a lawyer right away."

He made Maigret think of a ridiculous little mongrel which bares its teeth before anyone even begins to touch it.

"You seem very sure of being bothered."

"I must ask you not to speak to me again until my lawyer gets here. You can believe me when I say I'm sorry there's only one inn in this village."

Did he hear what the chief inspector muttered as he walked away?

"Cretin! Dirty little cretin!"

And Marie Tatin, without knowing why,

felt frightened to remain alone with him.

The day continued to the very end to be marked by confusion and indecision, probably because nobody felt qualified to take command.

Maigret, wrapped in his heavy coat, roamed around the village. At one time he was seen in the square in front of the church, at another in the vicinity of the chateau, where the windows lighted up one after another.

Night was falling fast. The church was brightly lighted and vibrating with the sound of the organ. The bell ringer locked the graveyard gate.

Groups of people who were scarcely visible in the darkness consulted one another. They did not know whether to call at the chateau to pay their respects to the dead woman. Two men went off to find out, and were received by the butler, who did not know what to do either. There was no tray ready for callers' visiting cards. He went to look for Maurice de Saint-Fiacre to ask what to do. The Russian woman said that he'd gone out for a breath of air.

She was lying on a bed, fully dressed, smoking a cigarette with a cardboard tip.

So the butler shrugged his shoulders and let the two callers in.

This was taken as a signal. After Vespers, there were more consultations.

"Yes, I tell you! Old Martin and young Bonnet have already been."

Everybody went together, in a procession. The chateau was poorly lighted. They walked along the hallway, silhouetted in turn against each window, pulling their children along by the hand or shaking them to stop them from making noise. The stairs . . . The next hallway . . . Finally, the bedroom, where these people would never have set foot before.

There was nobody there but the countess's maid, who watched the invasion in alarm. The farm people made the sign of the cross with a sprig of boxwood dipped in the holy water. The bolder spirits murmured in an undertone:

"You'd think she was asleep!"

And others echoed them:

"She didn't suffer."

Then their footsteps sounded on the uneven floor. The stairs creaked. There were murmurs of:

"Hush! . . . Hold the banisters tight. . . ."

The cook, in her basement kitchen, could see only the legs of the people passing by.

Maurice de Saint-Fiacre came back while the house was still full of people. He looked at them in wide-eyed surprise. The callers wondered if they ought to speak to him. But he just muttered something and went into Marie Vassilief's bedroom, where he could be heard talking in English.

Maigret, meanwhile, was in the church. The sacristan, holding the candle extinguisher, was going from taper to taper. The priest was taking off his vestments in the sacristy.

On both left and right were confessionals, with little green curtains to conceal the penitents. Maigret remembered the time when his face had not reached high enough to be hidden by the curtain.

Behind him, the bell ringer, who had not seen him, was bolting the main door.

The chief inspector suddenly crossed the nave and went into the sacristy, surprising the priest.

"Excuse me, Father, but I would like to ask you a question."

The priest's regular features wore a solemn expression, but it seemed to Maigret that his eyes were shining feverishly.

"This morning, something strange occurred here. The countess's missal, which was on her prayer stool, disappeared, and was later found hidden under the altar boy's surplice, in this very room."

Silence — only the sound of the sacristan's

footsteps on the carpet in the church, and the heavier footsteps of the bell ringer leaving through a side door.

"Only four people could have done that. . . . Please forgive me . . . The altar boy, the sacristan, the bell ringer . . ."

"And I!"

The voice was calm. The face was lighted on only one side, by a flickering candle flame. From a censer a thin wisp of blue smoke was spiraling toward the ceiling.

"It was . . . ?"

"It was I who took the missal and put it here, until such time . . ."

The ciborium, the altar cruets, and the sanctus bell were in their places, just as in the days when little Maigret had been an altar boy.

"Did you know what was inside the missal?"

"No."

"In that case . . ."

"I beg you not to ask me any more questions, Monsieur Maigret. I am under the seal of the confessional."

By an involuntary association of ideas, the chief inspector remembered his catechism. He also remembered the scene he had pictured when the old curé had told the story of a priest in the Middle Ages who had allowed his tongue to be torn out rather than break the seal of the confessional. He saw it again in every detail in his mind's eye, after more than thirty years.

"You know who the murderer is," he murmured, all the same.

"God knows who he is. . . . Excuse me. I have to go and see a sick person."

They went out through the rectory garden. A little gate separated it from the road. Some people who had come from the chateau were standing a little way off, discussing what had happened.

"You don't think, Father, that it's your place to . . ."

But they bumped into the doctor, who said, quietly:

"Father, don't you think this place is turning into something of a bawdyhouse? . . . Somebody ought to try to clean it up, if only to safeguard the people's morals! . . . Oh, so you're here too, Chief Inspector! Well, you've done some good work, I must say. At the moment, half the village is accusing the young count of . . . Especially since that woman arrived! . . . The manager is going to see the farmers to collect forty thousand francs, which, so it seems, are needed to . . ."

"Oh, go to blazes!"

Maigret walked away. He felt sick at heart.

Now he was accused of being the cause of all this trouble. What blunder had he committed? Indeed, what had he done? He would have given anything for a dignified atmosphere.

He strode along to the inn, which was half full, and caught one phrase:

"They say that if he can't find the money, he'll go to prison."

Marie Tatin was the picture of misery. She came and went, a busy little figure moving around like an old woman, although she was not more than forty.

"Is the lemonade for you? . . . Who ordered two beers?"

In his corner, Jean Métayer was writing, raising his head now and then to listen to the conversation.

Maigret went over to him. He could not read the cramped handwriting, but he saw that the paragraphs were clearly divided, had only a few corrections, and each was preceded by a number.

1 . . .

2 . . .

3 . . .

The secretary was preparing his defense while waiting for his lawyer to arrive.

A few feet away, a woman was saying:

"There weren't any clean sheets, and

they had to go and borrow some from the manager's wife."

Pale, with drawn features but a determined look in his eyes, Métayer wrote down:

4 . . .

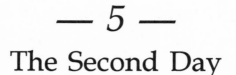

— 5 —

The Second Day

Maigret slept that restless yet voluptuous sleep you experienced only in a cold country bedroom that smells of cowshed, winter apples, and hay. Drafts were blowing all around him. And the sheets were icy, except in the one spot, a soft, cozy hollow, he had warmed with his body. So, rolled up in a ball, he avoided making the slightest movement.

Several times, he had heard Jean Métayer's dry cough in the next room. Then came the furtive footsteps of Marie Tatin, getting up.

He stayed in bed a few minutes longer. After he had lighted the candle, he didn't have the courage to wash with the icy water in the jug. He put off that operation until later, and went down in his slippers, without a collar.

Downstairs, Marie Tatin was pouring kerosene on the fire, which was refusing to catch. She had her hair in curlers, and she blushed when she saw the chief inspector come in.

"It isn't seven o'clock yet! The coffee isn't ready!"

Maigret had a small worry. Half an hour earlier, when he was half asleep, he thought he heard a car driving past. Saint-Fiacre is not on the main road. Almost the only traffic is the bus, which goes through the village once a day.

"The bus hasn't gone, has it, Marie?"

"Never before half past eight. And more often than not, nine o'clock . . ."

"Is that the bell for Mass ringing already?"

"Yes. It's at seven o'clock on regular days in the winter, and six o'clock in the summer. If you want to warm yourself . . ."

She pointed to the fire, which was finally burning well.

"You really can't bring yourself to call me *tu?*"

Maigret could have bitten his tongue off when he saw a coquettish smile appear on the poor woman's face.

"The coffee will be ready in five minutes."

It would not be full daylight before eight o'clock, and the cold was sharper than the day before. With his coat collar turned up, and his hat pulled down, Maigret walked slowly toward the bright patch of the church.

It was no longer a holy day. There were

no more than three women in the nave. And the Mass had something scamped and furtive about it. The priest went too quickly from one side of the altar to the other. He turned around too quickly too, with his arms outstretched, to mumble:

"Dominus vobiscum!"

The altar boy, who was having some difficulty in following him, said *Amen* at the wrong time.

Was panic going to set in again? He could hear the murmur of the liturgical prayers and now and then a gasp from the priest as he got his breath back between two words.

"Ite missa est . . ."

The three women stood up. The priest was reciting the last Gospel. Had this particular Mass lasted as much as twelve minutes?

A car drew up in front of the church, and soon hesitant footsteps could be heard outside.

Maigret had remained at the back of the nave, standing right by the door. Consequently, when it opened, the new arrival found himself literally face to face with the chief inspector.

It was Maurice de Saint-Fiacre. He was so surprised that he nearly beat a retreat, murmuring:

"I beg your pardon . . . I . . ."

But he took a step forward and made an effort to regain his composure.

"Is Mass over?"

He was obviously on edge. There were rings under his eyes, as if he had not slept a wink all night. And by opening the door, he had brought the cold air in with him.

"Have you come from Moulins?"

The two men were talking with forced politeness while the priest was reciting the prayer after the Gospel and the women were shutting their missals and picking up their handbags and umbrellas.

"How did you know? Yes . . . I . . ."

"Shall we go out?"

The priest and the altar boy had gone into the sacristy, and the sacristan was putting out the two tapers, which had been sufficient for this Low Mass.

Outside, the sky was lighter along the horizon. The white walls of the nearest houses stood out in the half-light. The yellow car was there, near the trees in the square.

Saint-Fiacre looked at Maigret, astonished perhaps at seeing him unshaven and without a collar.

"You got up early!" murmured the chief inspector.

"The first train, which is an express, leaves Moulins at three minutes past seven."

"I don't understand. . . . You didn't take the train, seeing that . . ."

"You're forgetting Marie Vassilief."

It was all so simple. And so natural. The presence of the count's mistress could only be an embarrassment at the chateau. So he had driven her to Moulins, put her on the train for Paris, and on his way back had dropped into the lighted church.

But Maigret was not satisfied. He was trying to follow the anxious glances of the count, who seemed to be waiting for somebody or to be afraid of something.

"She doesn't look like an easy person to deal with," hinted the chief inspector.

"She's known better days. So she's very sensitive. . . . The idea that I might want to hide our liaison . . ."

"Which has been going on for how long?"

"Just under a year . . . Marie doesn't care about money, but there have been difficult times."

His gaze had at last settled on one point. Maigret followed it and caught sight of the priest, who had just come out of the church. He had the impression that the two gazes met and that the priest was as embarrassed as the Count de Saint-Fiacre.

The chief inspector was about to speak to him, but with clumsy haste, the priest gave a rather curt greeting to the two men and went into the rectory as if he were running away.

"He doesn't look like a country priest."

The count made no reply. Through the lighted window, they could see the priest sitting down to his breakfast, and the housekeeper bringing him a steaming coffeepot.

Some small boys with satchels on their backs were beginning to make their way to school. The surface of Nôtre-Dame pond was beginning to look like a mirror.

"What arrangements have you made for . . ." began Maigret.

The other broke in far too quickly:

"For what?"

"For the funeral. Did anybody watch the body last night?"

"No. The idea was discussed for a few moments, but Gautier said that it wasn't done any more."

They heard the roar of a two-stroke engine in the courtyard of the chateau. A few moments later, a motorcycle went by, heading for Moulins. Maigret recognized Gautier's son, whom he had seen the day before. He was wearing a fawn raincoat and a checked cap.

Maurice de Saint-Fiacre did not know what to do with himself. He did not dare get back into his car. Yet he had nothing to say to the chief inspector.

"Has Gautier found the forty thousand francs?"

"No . . . Yes . . . I mean . . ."

Maigret looked at him inquisitively, surprised to see him so flustered.

"Has he found them or hasn't he? I got the impression yesterday that he was raising difficulties about it. Because, in spite of everything, in spite of all the mortgages and debts, you'll get much more than that amount . . ."

The count made no reply. He looked panic-stricken, for no apparent reason. And the next thing he said had no connection with the previous conversation.

"Tell me frankly, Chief Inspector, do you suspect me?"

"Suspect you of what?"

"You know perfectly well. . . . I've *got* to know."

"I have no more reason to suspect you than anybody else," Maigret replied evasively.

His companion leaped upon this statement.

"Thank you. . . . Well, that's what you must tell people. You understand? Otherwise, my position is impossible."

"What's the bank at which your check is going to be presented?"

"The Discount Bank."

A woman was heading for the wash house, pushing a wheelbarrow containing two baskets of laundry. The priest, in the rectory, was walking up and down, reading his breviary, but the chief inspector thought that he kept darting anxious glances at the two of them.

"I'll join you at the chateau."

"Now?"

"In a little while."

It was clear that Saint-Fiacre did not relish the idea at all. He got into his car like a condemned man. And the chief inspector could see the priest watching him drive away.

Maigret wanted to go and put on his collar at the very least. Just as he arrived at the inn, Jean Métayer came out of the grocer's. He had simply put a coat on over his pajamas. He looked at the chief inspector with a triumphant expression.

"A telephone call?"

The young man retorted acidly:

"My lawyer's arriving at ten to nine."

He was now sure of himself. He sent back some boiled eggs that were underdone and drummed his fingers on the table.

From the window of his bedroom, where he had gone to finish dressing, Maigret could see the courtyard of the chateau, the sports car, and Saint-Fiacre, who still did not seem to know what to do. Perhaps he was going to return to the village on foot.

The chief inspector hurried. A few moments later, he was walking toward the chateau. The two men met less than a hundred yards from the church.

"Where were you going?" asked Maigret.

"Nowhere. I don't know. . . ."

"Perhaps to say your prayers in the church?"

These few words were enough to make his companion turn pale, as if they had a mysterious, terrible meaning.

Maurice de Saint-Fiacre was not made for dramatic events. At first sight, he was a tall, strapping fellow, a magnificently healthy sportsman. If you looked more closely, you could see signs of his noble birth. Under the muscles, which were overladen with fat, there was hardly any energy. He had indeed probably had a sleepless night, and it seemed to have taken all the strength out of him.

"Have you had announcements of the death printed?"

"No."

"But what about the family . . . the local gentry . . . ?"

The young man lost his temper.

"They wouldn't come! You must know that! Before, yes. When my father was alive . . . During the shooting season, there were up to thirty guests at a time at the chateau, for weeks on end."

Maigret knew that as well as anybody. When there was a shoot, he had often, unknown to his parents, put on the white smock of a beater.

"Since then . . ."

The count made a gesture that signified: Things have gone from bad to worse.

The whole district must have talked about the crazy old woman, ruining the last years of her life with her so-called secretaries. And the farms being sold one after the other. And the son making a fool of himself in Paris.

"Do you think the funeral can be held tomorrow? . . . You understand; the sooner this situation comes to an end the better."

A cart full of manure went slowly by, its big wheels seeming to grind the pebbles on the road. The morning was grayer than the day before, but with less wind. In the distance, Maigret saw Gautier crossing the courtyard, coming toward them.

Then a strange thing happened.

"Will you excuse me?" the chief inspector said to his companion, and went off in the direction of the chateau.

He had gone scarcely a hundred yards when he turned around. Maurice de Saint-Fiacre was standing on the doorstep of the rectory. He must already have rung the door-bell. When he saw that he had been caught, he walked away quickly without waiting for a reply.

He did not know where to go. His whole bearing showed that he was terribly ill at ease. The chief inspector reached the manager, who had seen him coming and was waiting for him with an arrogant air.

"What do you want?"

"Just a piece of information. Have you found the forty thousand francs the count needs?"

"No. And I defy anybody to find them around here! Everybody knows just how much his signature is worth."

"So?"

"So he'll have to manage as best he can. It's not my business."

The count was retracing his steps. Maigret could tell he was longing to take a certain course of action, but for some reason it was impossible. Making up his mind, apparently, he came toward the chateau and stopped near the two men.

"Gautier! Come to the library for your in-structions."

He turned to go.

"I'll see you later on, Chief Inspector," he added with an effort.

When Maigret passed the rectory, he had the distinct impression that he was being watched through the curtains. But he could not be sure, because now that the sun had risen, the light inside had been put out.

There was a taxi standing outside Marie Tatin's. Inside the inn, a man of about fifty, immaculately dressed in striped trousers and a black, silk-edged jacket, was sitting at a table with Jean Métayer.

When the chief inspector came in, he jumped to his feet and rushed forward with outstretched hand.

"I understand that you are an inspector from the Police Judiciaire. Allow me to introduce myself: Maître Tallier, of the Bourges bar. . . . Will you have a drink with us?"

Métayer had stood up, but his face showed that he did not approve of his lawyer's cordiality.

"Innkeeper! Come and take our orders, please."

In a conciliatory voice he asked:

"What will you have? In this cold weather, what do you say to grog all around? . . . Three grogs, my good woman."

His "good woman" was poor Marie Tatin, who was unaccustomed to this manner of speaking.

"I hope, Chief Inspector, that you'll forgive my client. If I have understood him rightly, he has shown a certain mistrust of you. . . . But don't forget that he's a young man of good family, who has nothing on his conscience, and who was revolted by the suspicion he felt all around him. . . . The bad temper he displayed yesterday, if I may say so, is the best proof of his complete innocence."

With Maître Tallier there was no need to open your mouth. He took everything upon himself, questions and replies, accompanying his words with suave gestures.

"Of course, I don't know all the details. . . . If I have understood correctly, Countess de Saint-Fiacre died yesterday, during the first Mass, from heart failure. . . . Later, I gather, a piece of paper was found in her missal that suggests her death was due to a violent shock. . . . Did the victim's son — who, by a coincidence, happened to be in the vicinity — make a charge? . . . No! . . . In any case, I don't think that a charge would be accepted. The criminal act — if one took place — was not sufficiently clear-cut to justify the opening of an official inquiry.

"We are in agreement, are we not? No charge, so no legal action.

"Not that that prevents me from understanding the unofficial inquiries you are carrying out on your own . . .

"It isn't enough for my client not to be prosecuted. He must be cleared of all suspicion.

"Let me make myself clear. . . . What, after all, was his position at the chateau? That of an adopted son . . . The countess, left on her own, estranged from a son who caused her nothing but trouble, was comforted by her secretary's devotion and upright character.

"My client isn't an idler. He didn't just lead a carefree life, as he could have done at the chateau. He worked. He looked for investments. He even took an interest in recent inventions.

"Did he stand to benefit in any way from the death of his benefactress? . . . Need I say more? . . . I think not.

"And that, Chief Inspector, is what I want to help you to establish.

"I must add that there are a few indispensable measures that I shall have to take in conjunction with the solicitor. . . . Jean Métayer is a trusting soul. He never imagined that anything of this kind could happen.

"His belongings are at the chateau, mixed up with those of the late countess.

"Now, other persons have arrived there

who probably intend to lay their hands on . . ."

"A few pairs of pajamas and some old slippers!" growled Maigret, getting up.

"I beg your pardon?"

During the whole of this conversation, Métayer had been taking notes in a little notebook. It was he who calmed down his lawyer, who had stood too.

"Stop! I realized from the very first minute that I had an enemy in the chief inspector. And since then I have found that he belongs indirectly to the chateau. He was born at the time when his father was the Saint-Fiacres' estate manager. I warned you, Maître. It was you who insisted . . ."

It was ten o'clock. Maigret calculated that Marie Vassilief's train must have arrived half an hour earlier at the Gare de Lyon.

"Excuse me," he said. "I'll see you later."

"But . . ."

He in his turn went into the grocer's across the road, making the bell ring as he entered. He had to wait for a quarter of an hour to get through to Paris.

"Is it true that you're the old manager's son?"

Maigret was more tired than after ten normal cases. He felt utterly exhausted, both morally and physically.

"You're through to Paris."

"Hello. Is this the Discount Bank? This is the Police Judiciaire. Some information . . . Was a check signed Saint-Fiacre presented this morning? . . . What's that? . . . It was presented at nine o'clock and there were no funds to meet it? . . . Hello? . . . Don't cut us off, mademoiselle. You asked the bearer to present it again? . . . Excellent! . . . Ah, that's what I wanted to know. A young woman, wasn't it? . . . A quarter of an hour ago? . . . And she deposited the forty thousand francs? . . . Thank you . . . Yes, of course. Pay it . . . No, no, there's nothing wrong, seeing that the money's there."

Maigret came out of the booth heaving a weary sigh.

During the night, Maurice de Saint-Fiacre had found the forty thousand francs and he had sent his mistress to Paris to deposit them in the bank.

Just as the chief inspector was leaving the grocer's, he caught sight of the priest coming out of the rectory, with his breviary in his hand, and then heading for the chateau.

He quickened his pace, and almost ran to reach the door at the same time as the priest.

He missed by less than a minute. When he reached the courtyard, the door was closing

97

on the curé. And when he rang the bell, he heard footsteps at the far end of the hallway, going in the direction of the library.

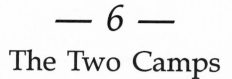

— 6 —

The Two Camps

"I'll see if Monsieur the Count can . . ."

But the chief inspector did not give the butler time to finish his sentence. He went into the hallway and made for the library while the butler gave a sigh of resignation. It was no longer possible to keep up appearances! People came and went as if they were in a shop. Things had come to a pretty pass.

Maigret paused before opening the library door, but it was in vain; he could not hear anything. Indeed, that was what made his entrance rather impressive.

He knocked, thinking that the priest might be somewhere else. But a voice, very firm and very clear in the silence of the room, replied immediately:

"Come in!"

Maigret pushed open the door, stepping accidentally on a heating vent. Facing him, leaning lightly against a Gothic table, was Count de Saint-Fiacre.

Beside him, staring at the carpet, the priest

remained absolutely still, as if the slightest movement might blow him away.

What were the two of them doing there, neither speaking nor moving? It would have been less embarrassing to interrupt a pathetic scene than to break into a silence so profound that the human voice seemed to trace concentric circles in it, like a pebble in a pool.

Once again, Maigret was conscious of Saint-Fiacre's weariness. As for the priest, he looked stunned, and his fingers were now twitching on his breviary.

"Excuse me for disturbing you."

His words sounded sarcastic, and yet he did not mean them to be. Was it possible to disturb people who were as inert as inanimate objects?

"I have some news from the bank."

The count's gaze moved to the priest and it was hard, almost furious.

The whole scene continued in the same vein. It was as if the characters were chess players thinking with their foreheads in their hands, remaining silent for several minutes before moving a pawn, and then returning to immobility.

But it was not thought that was immobilizing them like that. Maigret was convinced that it was fear of making a false move, a clumsy maneuver. Between the two of them there was a misunderstanding. And each one was reluctant to move his pawn, ready to take it back.

"I came to get instructions for the funeral," the priest felt it necessary to say.

That was not true. A pawn had been badly placed. So badly placed that Count de Saint-Fiacre smiled.

"I guessed that you would telephone the bank," he said. "And I am going to tell you why I decided to take that step. It was to get rid of Marie Vassilief, who did not want to leave the chateau. I persuaded her that it was absolutely essential."

In the priest's eyes now, Maigret could read anguish and disapproval.

The poor wretch, he must have been thinking, he has let himself be caught, he has fallen into the trap, he is done for.

Silence. Then the scraping of a match and puffs of smoke that the chief inspector blew out one after another as he asked:

"Gautier found the money?"

A very short pause.

"No, Chief Inspector . . . I'm going to tell you."

It was not on Saint-Fiacre's face that the drama was being enacted; it was on the priest's. He was pale. His lips had a bitter twist to them. He was making an effort not to intervene.

"Listen, Monsieur . . ."

He could not stand it any longer.

"Would you mind interrupting this conversation until we've had a talk?"

The same smile as before on the count's lips. It was cold in the huge room, from which the finest books in the library had been sold. A fire had been laid on the hearth; it just needed a match.

"Have you a lighter or . . ." the count said.

While he was bending over the hearth, the priest darted a miserable, beseeching look at Maigret.

"No," said the count, turning toward the others. "I'm going to clear up the situation in a few words. For some reason I don't know, the curé, who is full of good will, is convinced that it was I who — why should I be afraid of words? — who killed my mother! . . . For it was definitely a crime — wasn't it? — even if it doesn't quite fall within the jurisdiction of the law."

The priest was maintaining the trembling immobility of an animal which feels some danger approaching and cannot face it.

"The curé must have been very devoted to my mother. He probably wished to avoid the chateau's being involved in a scandal. . . .

Last night he sent the sacristan to me with forty thousand francs in cash, as well as a little note."

Without any possible doubt the expression in the priest's eyes was saying:

"Fool! You are done for!"

"Here is the note," Saint Fiacre went on. Maigret read in an undertone:

"Be careful. I am praying for you."

Whew! It was like the effect of a gust of fresh air. Immediately, Maurice de Saint-Fiacre ceased to feel condemned to one spot. He also lost his gravity, which was contrary to his nature. He started walking up and down, speaking in a lighter voice.

"That, Chief Inspector, is why you saw me prowling around the church and the rectory this morning. I accepted the forty thousand francs — which must obviously be regarded as a loan — first of all, as I have told you, to get my mistress out of the way — excuse me, Father — and then because it would have been extremely unpleasant to have been arrested right now. . . . But we are all standing, as if . . . Do sit down, please."

He went over to the door, opened it, and listened to a noise on the floor above.

"The procession is starting again," he murmured. "I think we'll have to telephone to Moulins to have a mortuary chapel installed." Then he went right on:

"I suppose you understand now? Once I had accepted the money, it remained for me to swear to the curé that I was not guilty. It was difficult for me to do that in front of you, Chief Inspector, without making you even more suspicious. . . . That's all! . . . This morning, as if you could read my thoughts, you didn't leave me alone for a moment in the vicinity of the church. Then the curé came here. I don't yet know why, because when you came in, he was hesitating to speak."

His eyes clouded over. To shake off the bitterness assailing him, he laughed, a painful laugh.

"It's simple, isn't it? A man who has led a 'loose' life and signed bad checks . . . Old Gautier is avoiding me! He too must be convinced that . . ."

Suddenly he looked at the priest with surprise.

"Well, Father, what's the matter?"

The priest, sure enough, looked even gloomier. His gaze avoided the young man's, and also tried to avoid Maigret's eyes.

Maurice de Saint-Fiacre understood, and exclaimed more bitterly:

"There you are! You still don't believe me.

And it's the very man who wants to help me who is convinced of my guilt."

He went and opened the door again and, forgetting the presence of the dead woman in the house, called out:

"Albert! . . . Albert! Look sharp, man! . . . Bring us something to drink."

The butler came in and went over to a cupboard, from which he took a decanter of whisky and some glasses. Nobody said anything. They watched him.

At last, Saint-Fiacre observed with a peculiar smile:

"In my time, there was no whisky in the chateau."

"It was Monsieur Jean . . ."

"Ah!"

He took a long drink, and then went and locked the door behind the butler.

"There are lots of things like that which have changed," he muttered to himself.

His eyes returned to the priest, and the latter, feeling increasingly ill at ease, stammered:

"Please excuse me, I must go to my catechism class."

"Just a moment . . . You are still convinced of my guilt, Father. . . . No, don't deny it. Priests are no good at lying. . . . But there are a few points I would like to clear up, because you don't know me; you weren't at Saint-Fiacre in my time, you've only heard people talking about me. . . . There are no material clues. The chief inspector, who was there when it happened, knows something about it."

"I beg you . . ." interrupted the priest.

"No! . . . You won't have anything to drink? . . . Good health, Chief Inspector!"

His face somber, he pursued his train of thought with fierce intensity.

"There are lots of people you could suspect. But it's I whom you suspect, and I alone. And I keep wondering why. That's what kept me from sleeping last night. I thought of all the possible reasons. Now, I think I know. . . . What did my mother tell you?"

This time the priest went white.

"I don't know anything."

"Come now, Father. You have helped me, I agree. You have let me have those forty thousand francs, which will grant me a breathing space and allow me to give my mother a decent burial. I thank you with all my heart. . . . Only, at the same time, you regard me with suspicion. You pray for me. That's either too much or not enough. . . ."

The voice began to take on a tone of anger and menace.

"I thought of having this talk with you outside Monsieur Maigret's presence. Well, now I'm glad that he is here. . . . The more I think about it, the more I detect something odd going on."

"Monsieur, I implore you not to torture me any more."

"And I, for my part, Father, warn you that you won't leave this room until you have told me the truth!"

He was a changed man. He was at the end of his tether, and, like all weak and gentle people, he had turned unduly fierce.

His voice must have been audible in the dead woman's room, which was just above the library.

"You were on good terms with my mother. I suppose Jean Métayer was one of your parishioners too. Which of the two said something? . . . My mother, wasn't it?"

Maigret remembered the words he had heard the day before:

"The seal of the confessional . . ."

He understood the priest's torment, his anguish, his martyred expression under the avalanche of Saint-Fiacre's words.

"What did she say to you? . . . I knew her, you know! I was present, so to speak, at the beginning of the decline. All of us here know what her life was like. . . ."

He looked around with unspoken anger.

"There was a time when people held their breath when they came into this room, because my father, *the master,* was working here. There was no whisky in the cupboards. But the shelves were loaded with books, as the cells of a beehive are saturated with honey. . . ."

Maigret remembered that too.

"The count is working. . . ."

And those words were enough to keep farmers waiting for two hours in the anteroom.

"The count called me into the library. . . ."

Maigret's father was impressed by this summons, because for him it was an important event.

"He didn't waste logs, but managed with a kerosene stove, which he put close to him, to help out the central heating," said Maurice de Saint-Fiacre.

And, speaking to the distraught priest, he went on:

"You never saw that. You saw the chateau only in decline. . . . My mother, who had lost her husband . . . whose only son was making a fool of himself in Paris and never came here except to ask for money . . . And then there were the secretaries. . . ."

His pupils were so bright that Maigret expected to see tears begin to flow.

"What did she say to you? . . . She was afraid of seeing me arrive, wasn't she? . . . She knew that there would be new debts to pay off, that something else would have to be sold to save me once again."

"You ought to calm down," the priest said in a dull voice.

"Not before knowing . . . whether you suspected me without knowing me, right from the start . . ."

Maigret intervened.

"The curé hid the missal," he said slowly.

He had by now understood. He was holding out a helping hand to Saint-Fiacre. He could imagine the countess, torn between sin and remorse. Wasn't she afraid of being punished? Wasn't she a little ashamed in front of her son?

She was a sick woman, easily worried. And it was quite possible that under the seal of the confessional she had said one day:

"I'm afraid of my son. . . ."

For she must have been afraid. The money that went to Jean Métayer and his like was Saint-Fiacre money, which rightly belonged to Maurice. Wouldn't he call her to account for it one day? Wouldn't . . ."

Maigret was conscious that these ideas were beginning to occur to the young man, though as yet in a confused form. He was helping to clarify them.

"The curé cannot say anything if the countess spoke under the seal of the confessional."

That was clear. Saint-Fiacre cut the conversation short.

"Forgive me, Father, I was forgetting your catechism class. . . . Please don't hold it against me if . . ."

He turned the key in the lock and opened the door.

"Thank you . . . As soon as . . . as soon as possible, I will return the forty thousand francs to you. I imagine they don't belong to you. . . ."

"I asked Madame Ruinard, the widow of the former solicitor, for them."

"Thank you . . . Good-bye."

He nearly slammed the door shut, but he restrained himself, looked Maigret in the eye and snarled:

"What a rotten business!"

"He wanted to . . ."

"He wanted to save me. I know! He tried to avoid a scandal, to stick the pieces of the chateau de Saint-Fiacre back together again as best he could. . . . It isn't that. . . ."

He poured some whisky.

"I'm thinking of that poor woman. . . .

Look, you've seen Marie Vassilief . . . and all the other women of Paris. They don't have attacks of conscience. . . . But my mother! . . . And remember that what she was looking for, above all else, with that fellow Métayer, was a chance to give her affection. . . . Then she would rush off to the confessional. She must have regarded herself as a monster. . . . From that to fearing my vengeance . . . Ha-ha! . . ."

His laughter was dreadful to hear.

"Can you see me, an indignant son, attacking my mother for . . . And that priest didn't understand! He sees life in terms of the Scriptures. While my mother was alive, he must have tried to save her from herself. Once she was dead, he thought it his duty to save me. . . . But at this moment I'm willing to bet he's convinced it was I who . . ."

He looked at the chief inspector and asked: "And what about you?"

When Maigret made no reply, he went on:

"For there has been a crime. A crime only the filthiest swine imaginable could have committed. . . . The dirty little coward! . . . Is it true that the law can do nothing against him? . . . I heard something to that effect this morning. But I'm going to tell you something, Chief Inspector, and you can take it down and use it against me: When I find that little swine — well, he'll have to deal with me, and me alone. . . . And I won't need a revolver! No. No weapon at all. Nothing but these two hands . . ."

The whisky was obviously making him more excited. Noticing that, he passed his hand over his forehead, looked in the mirror, and made a mocking face.

"The fact remains, if it hadn't been for the priest, I'd be in prison even before the funeral. I wasn't very nice to him. . . . And the wife of the former solicitor, who has paid my debt . . . who is she? . . . I can't remember."

"The lady who always dresses in white . . . The house that has a gate with gilded spikes, on the road to Matignon . . ."

Saint-Fiacre began to calm down. His outburst had been only a flash in the pan. He began to pour another drink for himself, hesitated, then swallowed the contents of his glass with a grimace of disgust.

"Can you hear that?"

"What?"

"The local people filing past upstairs . . . I ought to be there, in deep mourning, red-eyed, shaking their hands with a heartbroken air. . . . Once outside, they start talking."

He added suspiciously:

"Now I come to think of it, if, as you say,

the law is not concerned with the case, why are you staying here?"

"Something new might turn up."

"And if I found the culprit, would you prevent me from . . ."

The clenched fingers were more eloquent than any words.

"I must leave you," said Maigret. "I have to go and have a look at the other camp."

"The other camp?"

"The one at the inn. Jean Métayer and his lawyer, who arrived this morning."

"He's called in a lawyer?"

"He's a thoughtful fellow. This morning the two sides were lined up like this: at the chateau, you and the priest; at the inn, the young man and his adviser."

"You think he could have been capable . . . ?"

"May I help myself?"

And Maigret drank a glass of whisky, wiped his lips, and filled his pipe before leaving.

"I suppose you don't know how to use a linotype?"

A shrug of the shoulders.

"I don't know how to use anything. That's the trouble."

"You won't, under any circumstances, leave the village without informing me, will you?"

A grave deep look. And a grave, deep voice:

"I give you my word."

Maigret left. As he was about to go down the outside steps, a man appeared beside him before he could see where he had come from.

"Excuse me, Chief Inspector. Could you spare me a few minutes? . . . I've been told . . ."

"What?"

"That you practically belong to the house . . . Your father was in my job. . . . Would you do me the honor of having a drink with me in my home?"

The gray-bearded manager led his companion across the yard. Everything was ready in his house: a bottle of brandy whose label proclaimed its great age, biscuits. A smell of cabbage and bacon was coming from the kitchen.

"From what I've heard, you knew the chateau in very different circumstances. . . . When I arrived here, the decline was beginning. There was a young man from Paris who . . . This is brandy from the days of the late count. . . ."

Maigret stared at the table with the carved lions, which had brass rings in their mouths.

And once again he felt physically and morally tired. In the old days, he had been allowed to come into this room only if he was wearing slippers, because of the polished floor.

"I'm in a rather difficult position. . . . And it's you I'd like to ask for advice. We are poor people. You know that the manager's job doesn't make a man rich.

"Some Saturdays when there wasn't any money in the safe, I paid the farmers myself. . . .

"Other times, I advanced money to buy cattle the tenants wanted. . . ."

"In other words, the countess owed you money."

"Madame the Countess knew nothing about business. Money was disappearing all over the place. . . . It was only for indispensable things that it wasn't available."

"And it was you . . ."

"Your father would have done the same, wouldn't he? There are times when you mustn't let the local people see that the coffers are empty. I drew on my savings."

"How much?"

"Another glass? . . . I haven't counted. . . . At least seventy thousand . . . And now again, for the funeral, it's I who . . ."

A picture imposed itself on Maigret's mind:

His father's little office near the stables, at five o'clock on Saturday. All the people employed at the chateau, from the linen maids to the farm laborers, were waiting outside. And old Maigret, installed behind the desk covered with green percale, was arranging coins in little heaps. Each person passed by in turn and signed his name or made a cross on the register.

"Now I don't know how I'm going to get it back. . . . For people like us, it's . . ."

"Yes, I understand. . . . You've had the mantelpiece changed."

"Yes. The old one was wood. Marble looks better."

"Much better," grunted Maigret.

"You understand, don't you? All the creditors are going to descend on the chateau. . . . The count will have to sell. . . . And with the mortgages . . ."

The armchair in which Maigret was sitting was new, like the mantelpiece, and must have come from a Paris furniture shop. There was a phonograph on the sideboard.

"If I didn't have a son, I wouldn't mind, but Emile has his career to think about. . . . I don't want to rush matters."

A girl walked down the hallway.

"You have a daughter too?"

"No. That's a local girl, who comes in

to do the heavy work."

"Well, we'll talk about this another time, Monsieur Gautier. Excuse me. I still have a lot of things to do."

"Another glass?"

"No, thank you. You said about seventy-five thousand, didn't you?"

He left, his hands in his pockets, threaded his way through flocks of geese, and walked along beside Nôtre-Dame pond, where the water was no longer lapping. The church clock struck noon.

At Marie Tatin's, Jean Métayer and the lawyer were eating. They were having sardines, fillets of herring, and sausage, as hors d'oeuvres. On the next table were glasses that had contained their apéritifs.

The two men were in high spirits. They greeted Maigret with sarcastic glances and winked at each other. The lawyer's briefcase was closed.

"I hope you've at least found some truffles for the chicken," said Maître Tallier.

Poor Marie Tatin! She had found a tiny can of truffles at the grocer's, but she could not manage to open it, though she did not dare admit this.

"Yes, I've found some, monsieur."

"Then hurry up! The air here makes a man terribly hungry."

It was Maigret who went to the kitchen and, with his penknife, opened the can while the woman with the squint stammered in an undertone:

"I don't know what to say . . . I . . ."

"Be quiet, Marie!" he growled.

One camp . . . Two camps. . . Three camps?

He felt the need to make a joke, in order to forget the realities of the situation.

"By the way, the priest asked me to bring you three hundred days' indulgence. To count against your sins."

And Marie Tatin, who did not understand the joke, gazed at her burly companion with a mixture of fear and affectionate respect.

— 7 —

Meetings at Moulins

Maigret had telephoned to Moulins to order a taxi. He was surprised at first to see one arrive barely ten minutes after his telephone call, but as he was making for the door, the lawyer, who was just finishing his coffee, intervened.

"Excuse me! That's ours. But if you want a lift . . ."

"No, thank you."

So Jean Métayer and the lawyer left first, in a big car that still bore the coat of arms of its former owner. A quarter of an hour later, Maigret went off in his turn, and on the way, while he was chatting with the driver, he looked at the countryside.

The scenery was monotonous: two rows of poplars along the road, and plowed fields stretching away as far as the eye could see, with here and there a rectangular thicket or the blue-green eye of a pond.

The houses were for the most part just cottages. That was understandable, since there were no small landowners.

Nothing but big estates, one of which, that of the Duke de T————, contained three villages.

The Saint-Fiacre estate had covered seven and a half thousand acres before the successive sales.

The only means of transport was an old Paris bus, which had been bought by a farmer. It covered the distance between Moulins and Saint-Fiacre once a day.

"This is real country for you!" said the taxi driver. "It's all right now. But in the depths of winter . . ."

As they drove down the main street of Moulins, the hands of the clock of Saint-Pierre stood at half past two. Maigret asked the driver to stop in front of the Discount Bank and paid the fare. Just as he was turning away from the taxi, to go into the bank, a woman came out of the building holding a small boy by the hand.

The chief inspector hurriedly looked into a shop window, so as not to be noticed. The woman was a peasant woman in her Sunday best, her hat balanced on top of her hair. She was walking along in a dignified manner, trailing the boy behind her as though he were nothing but a parcel.

It was Ernest, the red-haired boy who served Mass at Saint-Fiacre.

The street was crowded. Ernest wanted to stop at each window, but he was towed along in the wake of the black skirt. Soon, however, his mother bent down to say something to him. And, as if it had been decided in advance, they went into a toy shop.

Maigret did not dare go too close. But he gathered what was happening from the whistle blasts that started coming from the shop. Every imaginable whistle was tried in turn. Finally, the altar boy must have decided on a whistle with two notes.

When he came out, he was wearing it on a string around his neck. His mother pulled him along again, preventing him from blowing it in the street.

It was a bank like any other in a small country town: a long oak counter, five clerks bent over desks. Maigret made for the section of the counter marked CURRENT ACCOUNTS, and one of the clerks stood up to serve him.

Maigret wanted to find out the exact state of the Saint-Fiacres' fortune, and, more important, what deposits or withdrawals were made in the last few weeks, or even the last few days. They might provide him with a clue.

But for a moment he said nothing, simply looked at the young man, who maintained a respectful attitude, showing no sign of impatience.

"Emile Gautier?"

He had seen him go past twice on a motorcycle, but he had been unable to distinguish his features. What revealed the bank clerk's identity to him was a striking resemblance to the manager of the chateau. Not so much a detailed resemblance as a resemblance to the same peasant origins: clear-cut features and big bones.

The same degree of evolution, more or less, revealed by skin rather better cared for than that of the farm workers, by intelligent eyes, and by the self-assurance of an "educated man."

But Emile was not yet a real city person. His hair, although covered with brilliantine, remained rebellious; it stood up in a point on top of his head. His cheeks were pink, with that well-scrubbed look of country yokels on Sunday morning.

"That is correct," he said.

He was not at all flustered. Maigret was sure that he was a model employee, in whom his manager had complete trust, and who would soon obtain promotion.

His black suit was made to measure, but by a local tailor, in a serge that would never wear out. His father wore a celluloid collar, but he wore a soft collar, with a ready-tied tie.

"Do you know me?" Maigret asked.

"No. I suppose you are the police officer . . ."

"I would like some information about the state of the Saint-Fiacre account."

"That's a simple matter. I am in charge of that account, as well as all the others."

He was polite, well mannered. At school, he must have been the teachers' favorite.

"Pass me the Saint-Fiacre account," he said to a girl clerk sitting behind him.

He let his gaze wander over a big sheet of yellow paper.

"Is it a summary you want, the amount of the balance, or some general information?"

At least he was precise.

"Is the account in a healthy state?"

"Come this way, will you? . . . Somebody might hear us here."

They went to the far end of the room, although still separated by the oak counter.

"My father must have told you that the countess was very unmethodical. . . . Time and again, I had to stop checks that could not be covered. Mind you, she didn't know that. . . . She used to make out checks without worrying about the state of her account. So when I telephoned to tell her, she would get into a panic. . . . This morning, again, three checks were presented, and I am obliged to return them. I have instructions to pay nothing until . . ."

"The family is completely ruined?"

"Not really. Several farms have been sold. Those remaining are mortgaged, like the chateau. The countess owned a block of flats in Paris, and that used to bring in a small income. But then, all of a sudden, she would throw everything off balance. . . . I've always done the best I could. I've had bills delayed two or three times. . . . My father . . ."

"Has advanced money. I know."

"That's all I can tell you. . . . At the moment, the balance stands at exactly seven hundred and seventy-five francs. . . . Mind you, last year's land tax hasn't been paid, and the collector issued a first warning last week."

"Is Jean Métayer aware of all this?"

"Yes. Indeed, more than just aware of it."

"What do you mean?"

"Nothing."

"You don't think he's living in the clouds?"

But Emile Gautier discreetly avoided making any reply.

"Is that all you want to know?"

"Are there any other inhabitants of Saint-Fiacre who have an account at this branch?"

"No."

"And nobody has been here today to transact any business? To cash a check, for example?"

"Nobody."

"And you have been here all the time?"

"I haven't moved from this counter."

He was in no way discomposed. He remained a good employee answering the questions of a government official with due courtesy.

"Would you like to see the manager? Not that he could tell you any more than I have . . ."

The streetlights were coming on. The main street was almost as crowded as in a big city, and there were long lines of cars in front of the cafés.

A procession went by: two camels and a young elephant carrying advertisements for a circus installed on Place de la Victoire.

In the grocer's shop, Maigret caught sight of the red-haired boy's mother, still holding her son by the hand. She was buying canned food.

A little farther on, he nearly bumped into Métayer and his lawyer, both walking along with a self-important air. The lawyer was saying:

". . . they are obliged to freeze it . . ."

They did not see the chief inspector, but continued on their way toward the Discount Bank.

People are bound to run into each other a dozen times in an afternoon in a town where all the activity is concentrated on a street five hundred yards long.

Maigret made his way to the *Journal de Moulins*. The offices were at the front of the building: a concrete façade with modern plate-glass windows holding a lavish display of press photographs and the latest news, written in blue pencil on long strips of paper.

"MANCHURIA. The Havas Agency reports that . . ."

But to reach the printing plant, Maigret had to go down a dark cul-de-sac, guided by the din of the rotary press. In a dismal room, some men in overalls were working at tall stone-topped tables. In a glass cage at the far end were the two linotypes, rattling like machine-guns.

"The foreman, please . . ."

He literally had to yell, over the thunder of the machines. The smell of ink took him by the throat. A short man in blue overalls who was arranging lines of type in a form cupped his hand around his ear.

"Are you the foreman?"

"Makeup man."

Maigret took from his wallet the piece of paper that had killed the Countess de Saint-Fiacre, which had been returned to him. The man settled steel-rimmed spectacles on his nose and looked at it, obviously wondering what this was all about.

"Was this printed here?"

"What?"

Some people went past carrying piles of newspapers.

"I asked you whether this was printed here."

"Come with me!"

It was better in the yard — cold, but at least they could talk in more or less normal voices.

"What were you asking me?"

"Do you recognize this type?"

"It's Cheltenham nine point."

"From here?"

"Nearly all linotypes have Cheltenham."

"Are there any other linotypes in Moulins?"

"Not in Moulins . . . but at Nevers, Bourges, Châteauroux, Autun, and . . ."

"Do you notice anything special about this piece of paper?"

"It's only a proof. Whoever did it wanted to make it look like a newspaper clipping, didn't they? . . . Somebody once asked me to do the same thing, for a joke."

"Oh?"

"At least fifteen years ago . . . In the days when we still set the newspaper by hand . . ."

"And the paper doesn't tell you anything?"

"Nearly all provincial newspapers have the same supplier. It's German paper. . . . Will you excuse me? I've got to lock up the form. It's for the Nièvre edition."

"Do you know Jean Métayer?"

The man shrugged his shoulders.

"What do you think of him?"

"If you take his word for it, he knows the business better than we do. He's kind of crazy. . . . We let him mess around in the plant because of the countess; she's a friend of the boss."

"Does he know how to work a linotype?"

"Hmm! . . . He says so."

"Well, would he be capable of setting this news item?"

"With a good two hours in front of him . . . and starting the same line over and over again . . ."

"Has he sat down at a linotype recently?"

"How do I know? He comes and goes all the time, bothering us with his pictures. . . . Excuse me. The train won't wait. And I haven't locked my form."

There was no point in persisting. Maigret nearly went back inside, but the frantic activity discouraged him. Every minute counted for these people. Everybody was running around. The porters elbowed him aside as they dashed toward the gate.

Yet he managed to buttonhole an apprentice, who was rolling a cigarette.

"What do you do with the lines of type when they've been used?"

"We melt them down."

"How often?"

"Every other day . . . Look! That metal pot over in the corner . . . Watch out! It's hot."

Maigret left, feeling weary, perhaps somewhat discouraged. Darkness had fallen. The street was bright, brighter than usual, because of the cold. Outside the tailor's shop, a salesman, who was stamping his feet and had a cold, was accosting passers-by.

"A winter overcoat? . . . Fine English cloth, from two hundred francs . . . Come inside! There's no obligation to buy."

A little farther on, outside the Café de Paris, where billiard balls could be heard colliding, Maigret saw Count de Saint-Fiacre's yellow car.

He went in, looked around for him and, failing to see him, sat down on a bench. It was the smart café of the town. On a platform, three musicians were tuning their instruments, after setting out the names of the next numbers with the help of three pieces of cardboard, each of which bore a figure.

There was the sound of a voice in the telephone booth.

"A beer," Maigret told the waiter.

"Light or dark?"

The chief inspector was trying to hear the voice in the booth. Just then Saint-Fiacre came out, and the cashier asked him:

"How many calls?"

"Three."

"To Paris, weren't they? . . . Three times eight is twenty-four. . . ."

The count caught sight of Maigret, walked over quite naturally, and sat down beside him.

"You didn't tell me you were coming to Moulins. I'd have driven you over in my car. It's true it's an open car, and in this weather . . ."

"Did you telephone Marie Vassilief?"

"No. I don't see why I should hide the truth from you . . . A beer for me too, waiter

130

. . . Or . . . no! Something hot. Grog . . . I telephoned a certain Monsieur Wolf. . . . If you don't know him, others at the Quai des Orfèvres are bound to. He's a money-lender. I've had recourse to him a few times. . . . I've just been trying to . . ."

Maigret looked at him inquisitively.

"You asked him for money?"

"At any rate of interest he liked! He refused, incidentally. . . . Don't look at me like that! I dropped into the bank this afternoon . . ."

"At what time?"

"About three o'clock . . . That young man and his lawyer were just coming out."

"You tried to withdraw some money?"

"I tried, yes! Now don't imagine that I want to arouse your pity. There are some people who get embarrassed by anything to do with money. I don't. . . . Well, after sending the forty thousand to Paris and buy-ing Marie Vassilief's ticket, I was left with about three hundred francs in cash. I arrived here without expecting anything like this to happen. . . . I've got nothing but the clothes I'm wearing now. . . . In Paris I owe a few thousand francs to the owner of my flat, and she won't send any of my things. . . ."

As he spoke he watched the balls rolling across the green cloth of the billiard table.

The players were humble young men of the town, who cast envious glances now and then at the count's elegant suit.

"That's all. I would at least have liked to be in mourning for the funeral. There isn't a tailor here who would give me credit for a couple of days. At the bank, I was told that my mother's account was frozen and that, in any case, the balance amounted to just over seven hundred francs. . . . And do you know who gave me that agreeable information?"

"Your manager's son."

"Right!"

He drank a mouthful of scalding grog and fell silent, still looking at the billiard table. The orchestra struck up a Viennese waltz, which was given a curious accompaniment by the sound of the balls.

It was hot. The light in the café was rather dim, in spite of the electric light. It was a typical provincial café, with only one concession to modern times, a notice advertising *Cocktails 6 francs.*

Maigret puffed slowly at his pipe. He too gazed at the billiard table, which was crudely lighted by lamps with green cardboard shades. Now and then the door opened, and after a few seconds a gust of icy air would reach him.

"Let's go and sit at the back . . ."

It was the voice of the lawyer from Bourges.

He passed by the table where the two men were sitting, followed by Jean Métayer, who was wearing white woollen gloves. But both of them were looking straight ahead. They did not see Maigret and the count until they had sat down.

The two tables were facing each other. There was a slight flush in Métayer's cheeks, and his voice trembled as he gave his order:

"Hot chocolate."

Saint-Fiacre commented jokingly in an undertone:

"That's right, darling!"

A woman sat down at an equal distance from the two tables, gave a friendly smile to the waiter, and murmured:

"The usual!"

He brought her a cherry brandy. She powdered her face, touched up her lipstick, and fluttered her eyelids, wondering which table to direct her gaze toward.

Was it burly, easygoing Maigret she ought to tackle? Or was it the more elegant lawyer, who was looking her up and down with a little smile?

"Well, I'll just have to lead the mourners in gray!" murmured the count. "After all, I can't very well borrow a black suit from the butler or put on one of my late father's tail coats!"

Apart from the lawyer, who was interested in the woman, everybody was looking at the nearest billiard table.

There were three tables. Two were occupied. There were a few cheers just as the musicians were finishing their number. And immediately the sounds of glasses and saucers could be heard again.

"Three ports!"

The door kept opening and shutting. The cold air came in and was gradually absorbed by the prevailing warmth.

The lamps over the third billiard table lighted up at a gesture from the cashier, who had the electric switches behind her.

"Thirty points!"

And speaking to the waiter, the same voice added:

"A quarter of Vichy . . . No! A strawberry Vittel . . ."

It was Emile Gautier, who was carefully coating the tip of his cue with blue chalk. Then he put the marker at zero. His companion was the assistant manager of the bank, a man ten years older, with a waxed mustache.

It was only at the third stroke — which he muffed — that the young man caught sight of Maigret. He greeted him, looking a little embarrassed. After that, he was so absorbed in the game that he no longer had time to notice anybody.

"If you're not afraid of the cold, I can give you a lift back in my car," said Saint-Fiacre. "May I offer you a drink? One apéritif more or less won't ruin me, you know."

"Waiter!" Métayer called out. "Get me Bourges seventeen on the telephone."

His father's number! A little later, he shut himself in the booth.

Maigret went on smoking. He had ordered another beer. And the woman, possibly because he was the fattest of the four men, had finally chosen him. Every time he turned in her direction, she smiled at him as if they were old acquaintances.

She could not have known that he was thinking about "the old girl," as the son himself called her, who was laid out on the second floor of the chateau back at Saint-Fiacre, with the farmers filing by her and nudging one another.

But it was not in those circumstances that he was picturing her. He was seeing her at a time when there were no cars yet in front of the Café de Paris and nobody drank cocktails there.

In the park of the chateau, a tall, lithe thoroughbred, like the heroine of a popular novel, beside the baby carriage being pushed along by the nursemaid . . .

Maigret was just a youngster, whose hair, like that of Emile Gautier and the red-haired altar boy, insisted on standing up in a point on top of his head.

Wasn't he jealous of the count that morning when the couple left for Aix-les-Bains in a motorcar (one of the first he had seen) full of furs and scent? The face behind the veil was invisible. The count was wearing huge goggles. It was all like a romantic elopement. And the nanny held the baby's hand and waved it in farewell.

Now they were sprinkling the woman with holy water and the bedroom smelled of candles.

Gautier circled the billiard table, played a fancy shot, and counted solemnly, in an undertone:

"Seven."

He bent down again, pulled off another shot. The assistant manager with the waxed mustache said in a sour voice:

"Magnificent!"

Two men eyed each other across the green cloth: Jean Métayer, to whom the smiling lawyer was talking incessantly, and Count de Saint-Fiacre, who stopped the waiter with an elegant gesture.

"The same again!"

Maigret was thinking of a whistle, a splendid bronze whistle with two notes, such as he had never possessed.

— 8 —

The Invitation to Dinner

"Another telephone call!" sighed Maigret as he saw Métayer stand up once more.

He followed him with his eyes, noting that he did not go into either the phone booth or the toilets. Moreover, the plump lawyer was now sitting on the very edge of his chair, like somebody who is wondering whether to get up. He was looking at Count de Saint-Fiacre. You might almost have thought that he was about to venture a smile.

Was it Maigret who was in the way? In any case, this scene reminded the chief inspector of certain incidents in his youth; three or four friends in a café together, and two women at the other end of the room. The discussions, the hesitations, the waiter you called to entrust him with a note . . .

The lawyer was in the same state of nervousness. And the woman sitting two tables away from Maigret misinterpreted it and thought that it was she who was responsible. She smiled, opened her handbag, and powdered her face.

"I'll be back in a moment," the chief inspector said to his companion.

He crossed the room in the direction Métayer had taken, and saw a door he had not noticed before, which led into a wide hallway with a red carpet. At the far end was a counter with a big book on it, a telephone switchboard, and a girl receptionist. Métayer was talking to her. He left her just as Maigret moved forward.

"Thank you, mademoiselle . . . You say it's the first street on the left?"

He made no attempt to hide from the chief inspector. He did not seem to be embarrassed by his presence. On the contrary! And there was a gleam of joy in his eyes.

"I didn't know that this was a hotel," Maigret said to the girl.

"You're staying somewhere else, then? . . . That's a pity. . . . Because this is really the best hotel in Moulins . . ."

"Haven't you had Count de Saint-Fiacre staying here?"

She nearly burst out laughing. Then she became serious all of a sudden.

"What's he done?" she asked with a certain anxiety. "That's the second time in five minutes that . . ."

"Where did you send the previous inquirer?"

"He wanted to know whether Count de Saint-Fiacre went out Saturday during the night. I couldn't tell him, because the night porter hasn't arrived yet. . . . Then the gentleman asked if we had a garage, and he's gone there."

So all that Maigret had to do was follow Métayer.

"And the garage is on the first street on the left," he said, a little annoyed in spite of everything.

"That's right. It's open all night."

Métayer had certainly lost no time, for when Maigret reached the street in question, he was coming out of the garage, whistling to himself. The attendant was eating a snack in one corner.

"It's for the same thing that gentleman has just asked you about . . . the yellow car. . . . Did anybody come and take it out Saturday night?"

There was a ten-franc note on the table. Maigret put down another.

"Yes, about midnight."

"And it was brought back?"

"About three o'clock in the morning."

"Was it dirty?"

"Not really . . . The weather's been dry lately, you know."

"There were two people, weren't there?

A man and a woman . . ."

"No! A man by himself."

"Short and thin?"

"Not at all. A big healthy fellow."

Obviously Count de Saint-Fiacre.

When Maigret went back into the café, the orchestra was playing again, and the first thing he noticed was that there was nobody left in the corner where Métayer and his companion had been sitting.

A few seconds later he spotted the lawyer sitting in his own seat, next to Count de Saint-Fiacre. At sight of the chief inspector he got up.

"Excuse me. No, do sit down here again, please."

He did not go away, however, but sat down on the chair opposite. Very nervous, his cheeks flushed, he was like a man in a hurry to be finished with a difficult task. His eyes seemed to be searching for Jean Métayer, who was nowhere to be seen.

"I want you to understand, Chief Inspector . . . I wouldn't have taken the liberty of going to the chateau — that goes without saying. But since we have been brought together by chance on neutral territory, if I may say so . . ."

And he gave a forced smile. After every

sentence, he gave the impression of bowing to the other two and thanking them for their approval.

"In a situation as painful as this, there is no point in complicating matters further, as I told my client, by being unduly sensitive. . . . Monsieur Jean Métayer understands this perfectly well. . . . And when you arrived, Chief Inspector, I was saying to Count de Saint-Fiacre that we asked for nothing better than to come to an understanding. . . ."

Maigret growled:

"Well, I'll be damned!"

And he thought:

You, my good fellow, will be lucky if in the next five minutes you don't get the hand of the gentleman you're talking to so suavely right across your face. . . .

The billiard players went on circling the tables. As for the woman, she stood up, leaving her handbag on the table, and went off toward the back of the room.

There's another who's making a big mistake, Maigret said to himself. She's just had a bright idea. Perhaps Métayer left the room so that he could speak to her outside without being seen? So off she goes to look for him. . . .

Maigret was right. With one hand on her hip, the woman was walking up and down, looking for the young man.

The lawyer was still talking.

"There are some very complicated interests involved, and we, for our part, are ready . . ."

"To do what?" Saint-Fiacre broke in.

"But . . . to . . ."

He forgot it was not his glass in front of him, and he drank out of Maigret's to keep himself in countenance.

"I know that perhaps this isn't the best place . . . or the best moment . . . but remember that we know better than anybody else the financial situation of . . ."

"My mother! Go on . . ."

"My client, with a tact that does him honor, decided to move into the inn. . . ."

The poor devil of a lawyer! His words, now that Maurice de Saint-Fiacre was gazing fixedly at him, were coming from his throat one by one, as if they needed to be dragged out.

"You do understand, don't you, Chief Inspector? . . . We know that there's a will in the lawyer's keeping. . . . Don't worry! The count's rights will be respected but Jean Métayer *is* a beneficiary. . . . The financial situation is rather complicated. My client is the only one who knows all about it. . . ."

Maigret admired Saint-Fiacre, who was

managing to maintain an almost angelic composure. There was even a faint smile on his lips.

"Yes! He was a model secretary," he said without any apparent irony.

"You must remember that he comes from a very good family and has had an excellent upbringing. I know his parents. . . . His father . . ."

"Let's get back to the fortune, shall we?"

It was too good to be true. The lawyer could scarcely believe his ears.

"Will you allow me to offer you both drinks? . . . Waiter! The same again, gentlemen? . . . As for me, I'll have a lemon Raphaël."

Two tables away, the woman had returned glumly to her seat; she had failed to find Métayer and had resigned herself to tackling the billiard players.

"I was saying that my client is prepared to help you. There are certain persons whom he distrusts. He'll tell you himself that some rather shady operations have been carried out by people not overburdened with scruples. . . . Anyway . . ."

This was the most difficult part. In spite of himself, the lawyer had to swallow hard before going on.

"You've found the chateau coffers empty.

. . . But it's essential for your late lamented mother . . ."

"Your late lamented mother!" Maigret murmured admiringly.

"Your late lamented mother," the lawyer repeated without batting an eyelid. "What was I saying? . . . Oh, yes! That the funeral should be worthy of the Saint-Fiacres. . . . Pending the time when matters can be arranged in everybody's best interest, my client will see to it that . . ."

"In other words, he will advance the money necessary for the funeral. Is that what you mean?"

Maigret did not dare look at the count. Fixing his gaze on Emile Gautier, who was making another break, he waited tensely for the explosion about to take place beside him.

But no! Saint-Fiacre had stood up. He was speaking to a new arrival.

"Do sit down at our table, monsieur."

It was Métayer, who had just come in and to whom the lawyer had doubtless explained by signs that everything was going well.

"A lemon Raphaël too? . . . Waiter!"

Applause broke out in the room, because the orchestra's set was over. Once the noise had died down, the situation was more embarrassing, for voices sounded louder. There was now only the click of the ivory balls to break the silence.

"I told the count, who understands perfectly . . ."

"Who is the Raphaël for?"

"You came from Saint-Fiacre, didn't you, gentlemen? . . . In that case, my car is at your disposal to take you back. You'll find it rather a tight fit. I'm giving a lift to the chief inspector. . . . How much, waiter? . . . No, please! It's my round."

But the lawyer stood up and was pressing a hundred-franc note into the hand of the waiter, who asked:

"All of them?"

"Yes, yes!"

And the count said with his most gracious smile:

"It's really too charming of you."

Emile Gautier, watching the four of them leave, making way for each other at the door, was so surprised he forgot to go on with his break.

The lawyer found himself in front, next to the count, who was driving. Behind, there was only just enough room for Métayer beside Maigret.

It was cold. The headlights were not bright enough. The car had no muffler, and this made conversation impossible.

Did Maurice de Saint-Fiacre usually drive at this speed? Or was he taking his little revenge? The fact remains that he covered the fifteen miles from Moulins to the chateau in less than a quarter of an hour, braking on the curves, speeding through the darkness, and once only narrowly missing a cart, which was in the middle of the road and thus forced him to drive up on the bank.

Their faces were cut by the wind. Maigret had to grip the collar of his coat in both hands. They drove through the village without slowing down. It was as much as they could do to catch a glimpse of the light in the inn and then the church spire.

A sudden stop, which threw the occupants of the car against one another. They were at the foot of the steps. The servants could be seen eating in the basement kitchen. Somebody was roaring with laughter.

"Will you allow me, gentlemen, to invite you to dinner?"

Métayer and the lawyer looked at each other in hesitation. The count pushed them inside with a friendly tap on the shoulder.

"Come along now . . . It's my turn, isn't it?"

And in the hall he added:

"Unfortunately, it won't be very festive."

Maigret would have liked to have a few words with him in private, but the other did not give him time and opened the door of the smoking room.

"Will you excuse me for a few moments? I have some orders to give. Have an apéritif while you're waiting. You know where the bottles are, don't you, Monsieur Métayer? . . . Is there anything drinkable left?"

He pressed an electric bell push. The butler was a long time coming, and arrived with his mouth full and his napkin in his hand.

Saint-Fiacre snatched it from him with a swift gesture.

"Send for the manager . . . Then get me the rectory and the doctor's house on the telephone."

And to the others he said again:

"Will you excuse me?"

The telephone was in the hall, which, like the rest of the chateau, was poorly lighted. Since there was no electricity in Saint-Fiacre, the chateau had to provide its own current, and the generator was too weak. The bulbs, instead of giving off a white light, revealed reddish filaments, as they do in some streetcars when they come to a halt.

The hall was full of great patches of dark shadow in which it was almost impossible to make out objects.

"Good evening . . . Yes, I insist. . . . Thank you, Doctor . . ."

The lawyer and Maigret were uneasy. But they did not dare admit their uneasiness to each other. It was Métayer who broke the silence, to ask the chief inspector:

"What can I offer you? I don't think there's any port left. But there's some whisky. . . ."

All the ground-floor rooms were in a row, separated by wide-open doors. The dining room first. Then the drawing room. Then the smoking room, where the three men were waiting. And finally the library, where the young man went to get the drinks.

"Good evening . . . Yes . . . Can I count on you? . . . I'll expect you soon . . ."

The count made more calls, then walked down the hallway running alongside all the rooms and went upstairs, where his footsteps stopped in the dead woman's bedroom.

Other, heavier, footsteps sounded in the hall. A knock came on the door, which opened right away. It was old Gautier.

"You wanted to see me?"

Then he noticed that the count was not there, looked in astonishment at the three people in the room, and beat a retreat, questioning the butler outside.

"Soda?" asked Métayer.

And the lawyer, full of good will, began

with a little cough:

"We both of us have queer professions, Chief Inspector. . . . Have you been in the police force a long time? . . . I've been at the bar for nearly fifteen years. So you can imagine that I've been mixed up in the most astonishing cases. . . . Good health! . . . Here's to you, Monsieur Métayer. I'm glad, for your sake, about the turn events are taking."

The count could be heard in the hall saying:

"Well, you must find some! Telephone your son, who is playing billiards at the Café de Paris in Moulins. He'll bring along what's necessary."

The door opened. The count came in.

"You've found something to drink? . . . Aren't there any cigars here?"

He looked inquiringly at Métayer.

"Cigarettes. I only smoke . . ."

The young man did not finish what he was saying, but turned his head away in embarrassment.

"I'll bring you some."

"Gentlemen, I hope you'll excuse the very modest meal you're going to eat. We are a long way from town and . . ."

"Come," said the lawyer, on whom the whisky was beginning to take effect. "I'm sure it will be excellent. . . . Is that a relative of yours?"

He pointed to a portrait on the smoking-room wall of a man dressed in a stiff frock coat, his neck imprisoned in a starched collar.

"That is my father."

"Yes, you take after him."

The servant showed in Dr. Bouchardon, who looked around distrustfully, as if he suspected a plot of some sort. But Saint-Fiacre received him gaily.

"Come in, Doctor . . . I presume you know Jean Métayer. . . . His lawyer; a charming man, as you'll see . . . As for the chief inspector . . ."

The two men shook hands, and a few moments later the doctor growled in Maigret's ear:

"What have you cooked up here?"

"I haven't. *He* has."

To retain his composure, the lawyer kept going to the little table where he had put his glass, and he did not realize that he was drinking more than usual.

"This old chateau is an absolute gem. And what a setting for a film! . . . That's what I was saying only the other day to the public prosecutor at Bourges, who loathes motion pictures. As long as they go on shooting

151

films in settings that . . ."

He was talking too excitedly, and constantly trying to capture someone's attention.

As for the count, he had gone over to Métayer and was showing a disturbing affability towards him.

"The saddest thing here is the long winter evenings. True . . . *In my time,* I remember that my father, too, was in the habit of inviting the doctor and the priest. . . . They weren't the same ones as now. But the doctor was a skeptic, and the conversation always ended by turning to philosophical subjects. . . . Well, speak of the devil . . ."

It was the priest, with rings under his eyes and an embarrassed manner, who did not know what to say and was standing hesitantly in the doorway.

"Excuse me for being late, but . . ."

Through the open doors they could see two servants laying the table in the dining room.

"Do offer Father something to drink."

It was to Métayer that the count was speaking. Maigret noticed that the latter was not drinking, but the lawyer was well on the way to being drunk. He was explaining to the chief inspector:

"A little diplomacy, that's all! Or, if you like, knowledge of human nature . . . They're about the same age, and both from good families. Can you think of any reasons why they should have failed to hit it off? Aren't their interests related? . . . The curious thing —" he laughed, took another gulp of whisky "— is that it happened accidentally in a café. There's a lot to be said for those good old provincial cafés, where you feel as though you were at home."

They had heard the sound of an engine outside. A short time later the count went into the dining room, where the manager was, and they caught a few words:

"Both of you, yes. . . . If you like . . . that's an order!"

The telephone rang. The count had rejoined his guests. The butler came into the smoking room.

"The undertaker . . . He wants to know when he can bring the coffin."

"Whenever he likes."

"Very well, monsieur."

And the latter said, almost cheerfully:

"Shall we go in to dinner? I've had the last bottles in the cellar brought up. . . . After you, Father . . . We're a little short of feminine company, but . . ."

Maigret tried to hold him back by his sleeve. The other looked him in the eyes with a hint of impatience, then disengaged himself abruptly and went into the dining room.

"I've invited Monsieur Gautier, our estate manager, and his son, a young man with a promising future, to share our meal."

Maigret looked at the bank clerk's hair, and, in spite of his uneasiness, he could not help smiling. The hair was wet. Before coming to the chateau, the young man had checked the part, washed his face and hands, and changed his tie.

"Let's sit down, gentlemen."

And the chief inspector could have sworn that a sob rose in Saint-Fiacre's throat. It went unnoticed because the doctor involuntarily distracted everyone's attention by seizing a dusty bottle and murmuring:

"So you still have some Hospices de Beaune 1896? I thought that the last bottles were bought by the Restaurant Larue and that . . ."

The rest was drowned by the sound of chairs being moved. The priest, his hands folded on the tablecloth, his head bent, his lips moving, said grace.

Maigret surprised Saint-Fiacre's gaze fixed intently on him.

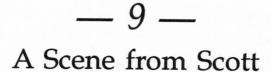

— 9 —

A Scene from Scott

The dining room was the part of the chateau that had lost the least of its character, thanks to the carved paneling that covered the walls up to the ceiling. Moreover, the room was high rather than large, and this made it not only solemn, but also gloomy; guests felt like they were eating at the bottom of a well.

On each panel were two electric lights, imitation candles, which even had artificial beads of wax.

In the middle of the table was a real candelabrum, with seven branches and seven real candles.

Count de Saint-Fiacre and Maigret were sitting face to face, but could see each other only if they strained their necks to look over the flames.

On the count's right was the priest; on his left, Dr. Bouchardon. Chance had placed Jean Métayer at one side of the table, his lawyer at the other side. Next to the chief inspector there was the steward on one hand, Emile Gautier on the other.

The butler occasionally advanced into the light to serve the guests, but as soon as he took two paces back he was lost in the shadows, and nothing could be seen of him but his white-gloved hands.

"Wouldn't you think we were in one of Walter Scott's novels?"

It was the count who was speaking, in a casual voice. And yet Maigret pricked up his ears; he sensed an underlying meaning, guessed something was beginning.

They were only at the hors d'oeuvres. On the table, all mixed up, were a score of bottles of red and white wine, clarets and burgundies. Each person helped himself.

"There's only one detail that is missing," Maurice de Saint-Fiacre went on. "In Walter Scott, the poor old girl upstairs would suddenly start screaming."

For a few seconds, everybody stopped eating. They felt something like a draft of icy air pass by.

"Incidentally, Gautier, has she been left alone?"

The manager swallowed hurriedly, and stammered:

"She . . . Yes . . . There's nobody in the countess's room."

"It can't be very cheerful."

At that moment a foot pressed hard against

Maigret's, but the chief inspector could not guess whose it was. The table was a round one. Each person could reach past the center. And Maigret's uncertainty was due to continue, since during the evening the little kicks would follow one another with increasing frequency.

"Has she received many callers today?"

It was embarrassing to hear him talking like that of his mother, as if she were alive, and the chief inspector noticed that Métayer was so upset that he stopped eating and stared straight ahead, his face more and more haggard.

"Nearly all the local farmers," came the reply, in Gautier's deep voice.

Whenever the butler noticed a hand reaching out toward a bottle, he would step forward noiselessly. His black arm, with a white glove at the end of it, would appear. The liquid would flow. This was done so silently and skillfully that the lawyer, already more than a little drunk, admiringly set the operation going three or four times.

He followed that arm with fascination, noting that it did not even brush against his shoulder. Finally he could contain himself no longer.

"Marvelous! Butler, you're a wizard, and

if I could afford a chateau, I'd take you into my service."

"Well, the chateau will be up for sale soon, and at a low price."

This time Maigret frowned as he looked at Saint-Fiacre, who had spoken in a strange voice, casual yet a little theatrical. And there was something irritating about his remark. Was he too much on edge? Was this a sinister form of humor?

"Chicken in half-mourning," he announced as the butler brought in a dish of chicken with truffles.

Then he went straight on, in the same light-hearted voice:

"The murderer is going to eat some chicken in half-mourning, like the rest of us!"

The butler's arm slipped backward and forward between guests. The manager's voice said, in a tone of comic horror:

"Oh, Count . . ."

"Why yes! What is so extraordinary about that? The murderer is here; that's certain! But don't let that take away your appetite, Father. The corpse is in the house, too, and that isn't preventing us from eating. . . . A little wine, Albert, for the curé."

The foot brushed against Maigret's ankle again. The chief inspector dropped his napkin and bent down to look under the table, but too late. When he straightened up again, the count, continuing to eat his chicken, was saying:

"I mentioned Walter Scott just now because of the atmosphere in this room, but also, and above all, because of the murderer. After all, this is a funeral wake. . . . The funeral takes place tomorrow morning, and in all probability we shall stay together until then. . . . It must at least be said to Monsieur Métayer's credit that he has filled the liquor cabinet with some excellent whisky. . . ."

Maigret tried to remember how much Saint-Fiacre had drunk. Less, in any case, than the lawyer, who exclaimed:

"Yes, excellent! There's no doubt about that. But then my client is the grandson of vine-growers. . . ."

"As I was saying . . . But what was I saying? . . . Oh, yes! . . . Fill up the curé's glass, Albert. . . .

"As I was saying, since the murderer's here, the others find themselves, so to speak, cast in the role of judges. And that is what makes our dinner party resemble something out of Walter Scott.

"Though you must remember that the murderer in question isn't really in any danger. Isn't that so, Chief Inspector? . . . It isn't a crime to slip a piece of paper into a missal.

159

"While we are on the subject, Doctor . . . when did my mother's last attack take place?"

The doctor wiped his mouth and looked around him with a disgruntled expression.

"Three months ago, when you wired from Berlin that you were ill in a hotel room and that . . ."

"I wanted some cash. That's it!"

"I observed at that time that the next violent shock would be fatal."

"So that . . . let's see . . . Who knew that? . . . Jean Métayer, of course. I myself, obviously. Old Gautier, who is almost one of the family. And you and the curé."

He drank a whole glass of Pouilly, then grimaced.

"This is just to explain to you that, logically speaking, we can nearly all be considered suspects. . . . If the idea amuses you . . ."

It was as if he were deliberately choosing the most shocking words he could.

"If the idea amuses you, we can go on to examine the case of each person separately. . . . Let us begin with the curé: Had he anything to gain by killing my mother? . . . You are going to see that the answer is not as simple as it may appear. I leave the question of money to one side."

The priest was choking with indignation

160

and hesitating over whether to leave the table.

"The curé had nothing to hope for in that respect. But he is a mystic, an advocate, almost a saint. He has an odd parishioner whose conduct is a source of scandal. Sometimes she rushes to church like the most fervent of the faithful, but at other times she brings scandal to Saint-Fiacre. . . . No, don't make that face, Métayer. We're all men here. We are, if you like, engaged in advanced psychology. . . .

"The curé has such fierce faith that it might push him to extreme measures. Remember the times when sinners were burned to purify them . . . My mother is at Mass. She has just taken Communion. She is in a state of grace. . . . But, very soon, she is going to fall back into her sinful ways and be a source of scandal once more. . . .

"Whereas, if she dies a holy death, there in her pew . . ."

"But . . ." began the priest, who, with tears in his eyes, was holding on to the table.

"Don't take offense, Father. We are simply talking about psychology. I want to show you that the most austere people can be suspected of the worst outrages. . . . If we go on now to the doctor, I'm in a more difficult position. He isn't a saint. And, fortunately for him, he isn't even a savant. If he were,

161

he might have put the piece of paper in the missal as an experiment, to test the resistance of a weak heart. . . ."

The sound of forks had slowed to such an extent that it had nearly dropped to nothing. And the guests' eyes were fixed, uneasy, even haggard. Only the butler was unmoved, and went on filling the glasses in silence, with the regularity of a metronome.

"You look gloomy, gentlemen. Is it really not possible for us, as intelligent people, to broach certain subjects?

"Serve the next course, Albert . . . So we put the doctor aside, seeing that we cannot regard him as a savant or a researcher. He is saved by his mediocrity. . . ."

He gave a little laugh and turned toward old Gautier.

"Your turn now . . . A more complicated case . . . There are two possibilities. First, you are the model manager, the upright man who devotes his life to his masters and the chateau where he was born and bred. You weren't born and bred here, but that doesn't matter. In this case, your position isn't clear. The Saint-Fiacres have only one male heir. And little by little the family fortune is rapidly disappearing under the nose of that heir. The countess is behaving like a lunatic. . . . Isn't it time to save what's left?

"Now that's as noble as anything in Walter Scott, and your case resembles that of the curé.

"But there's the opposite hypothesis to be considered too. You are no longer the model manager born and bred at the chateau. You are a scoundrel, and for years you've been taking advantage of your masters' weakness. When mortgage money is needed, it's you who raise it. . . . Now don't lose your temper, Gautier. The curé didn't lose his, did he? . . . And I haven't finished yet.

"You are practically the real owner of the chateau. . . ."

"Monsieur!"

"Don't you know how to play the game? Because, I tell you, we are playing a game! We are playing, if you like, at all being chief inspectors like your neighbor. . . . The time has come when the countess has her back to the wall, everything will have to be sold, and she will find out that it's you who will profit from the situation. . . . Wouldn't it be better for the countess to die conveniently, which would also save her from making the acquaintance of poverty?"

And, turning toward the butler, a shadow in the shadows, a demon with two chalk-white hands, he said:

"Albert! Go and fetch my father's revolver

. . . That is, of course, if it's still here."

He poured some wine for himself and for his two neighbors, then passed the bottle to Maigret.

"Will you do the serving on your side? . . . Well! We've almost got halfway through our little game. . . . But let's wait for Albert. . . . Monsieur Métayer, you aren't drinking."

They heard a strangled "No, thank you."

"How about you, Maître?"

The latter, his mouth full, his tongue coated, replied:

"No, thank you! No, thank you! I have everything I need. . . . You'd make a wonderful public prosecutor, you know."

He was the only one to laugh, to eat with indecent gusto, and to drink glass after glass, sometimes burgundy, sometimes claret, without even noticing the difference.

They heard the tinny bell of the church clock strike ten. Albert handed a heavy revolver to the count, and the latter checked that it was loaded.

"Perfect! I'll put it here, in the middle of the table. . . . You will notice, gentlemen, that because this is a round table, it is at an equal distance from each person. . . . We have examined three cases. Now we are going to examine three more. But first, will you

164

allow me to make a prophecy? . . . To remain in the Walter Scott tradition, I foretell that before midnight my mother's murderer will be dead!"

Maigret darted a sharp glance at him across the table, and saw a pair of eyes that were shining brightly, as if Saint-Fiacre was drunk. At the same moment, a foot touched his again.

"And now I'll go on. . . . But do eat your salad . . . I come now to your neighbor, Chief Inspector, on your left; that is to say, Emile Gautier. A serious, hard-working young man, who, as they say at school prize days, has made his way by merit and sheer hard work. . . .

"Could he have killed my mother?

"One hypothesis: he worked hand in glove with his father, for his father. . . .

"He goes every day to Moulins. He knows the financial situation of the family better than anybody else. He has every opportunity of seeing a printer or a linotype operator. . . .

"Let's go on . . . Second hypothesis. You'll forgive me for telling you, Métayer, if you don't know already, that you had a rival. Emile Gautier is no beauty. All the same, he preceded you in the position you occupied with such tact.

"That was a few years ago. Did he begin to entertain certain hopes? Had he succeeded, since then, in stirring my mother's tender heart once more?

"The fact remains that he was her official protégé, and that he was entitled to conceive all sorts of ambitions. . . .

"You came. You conquered.

"Why not kill the countess and at the same time throw suspicion on you?"

Maigret's toes stirred uncomfortably in his shoes. All this was horrible, sacrilegious! Saint-Fiacre was talking as excitedly as a drunkard. And the others were wondering whether they could stick it out to the end, whether they should stay and endure this scene or get up and go.

"You can see that we are faced with a complete mystery. . . . Mind you, the countess herself, up there, if she could speak, would be unable to give us the solution to the problem. The murderer is the only person who knows about his crime. . . . Eat up, Emile . . . and don't let this upset you, like your father, who seems to be on the verge of fainting.

"Albert! There must be a few bottles of wine left in the bin somewhere.

"Your turn now, young man!"

And he turned with a smile to face Métayer,

166

who jumped to his feet.

"Monsieur, my lawyer . . ."

"Sit down, dammit! And don't make us think that at your age you can't take a joke."

Maigret was watching him while he was saying this, and he noticed that the count's forehead was covered with large beads of sweat.

"None of us is trying to make himself out to be better than he is, is he? . . . Good! I see that you are beginning to understand. Have some fruit. It's excellent for the digestion."

It was unbearably hot, and Maigret wondered who had switched off the electric lights, leaving only the candles on the table burning.

"Your case is so simple that it's positively uninteresting. . . . You were playing a not very amusing part, which nobody is willing to play for very long. Still, you were in my mother's will. . . . That will risked being changed at any moment. A sudden death, and it would be all over. You would be free! You would harvest the fruits of your . . . of your sacrifice. And, dammit all, you would be able to marry some young girl you must have waiting for you back home."

"I beg your pardon!" the lawyer protested, so comically that Maigret could not help smiling.

"Shut your mouth! Drink up!"

Saint-Fiacre was categorical. He was drunk; there could no longer be any shadow of a doubt about that. He was displaying the eloquence peculiar to drunkards, a mixture of brutality and subtlety, of facile eloquence and blurred speech.

"I'm the only one left!"

He called Albert.

"Look, old fellow, go upstairs. It must be so dismal for my mother, staying all alone."

Maigret saw the butler glance inquiringly at old Gautier, who gave a little nod.

"Just a moment! Bring us a few bottles first . . . the whisky, too. Nobody objects to a little informality, I imagine."

He looked at his watch.

"Ten past eleven . . . I've been talking such a lot that I haven't heard your church clock, Father."

When the butler moved the revolver slightly while putting the whisky decanters on the table, the count said:

"Careful, Albert! It must remain at an equal distance from each of us."

He waited until the door was closed.

"There!" he said. "I'm the only one left! I won't be telling you anything new when I say I've never done anything worthwhile. Except, perhaps, in my father's lifetime.

168

But since he died when I was only seventeen . . .

"I'm on the rocks. Everybody knows that.
The popular press makes no secret of the
fact.

"I sign bad checks. I try my mother for
a loan as often as I can. I invent illness in
Berlin to get a few thousand francs. . . .

"You will notice that that was the missal
trick on a smaller scale.

"Now, what's happening? . . . The money
that is due to come to me someday is being
spent by little swine like Métayer. . . . Excuse me, young man . . . This is still tran-
scendental psychology. . . .

"Soon there'll be nothing left. I telephone
my mother, at a time when a bad check is
just about to land me in prison. She refuses
to pay. There are witnesses who can testify
to that.

"Besides, if this goes on, there'll be nothing
left of the family fortune in a short time.

"Two hypotheses, as in the case of Emile
Gautier. The first . . ."

Never in his whole career had Maigret felt
so uncomfortable. And it was probably the
first time he had had the definite feeling of
being incapable of dealing with the situation.
Events were leaving him behind. Now and
then he thought he understood, and the next

moment a phrase of Saint-Fiacre's would make him question everything again.

And all the time there was that insistent foot pressing against his.

"Let's change the subject!" suggested the lawyer, who was now completely drunk.

"Gentlemen," began the priest.

"I beg your pardon. You must bear with me until midnight at least. I was saying that the first hypothesis . . .

"Damn! Now you've made me lose the thread of my idea. . . ."

As if to help himself find it again, he poured himself a full glass of whisky.

"I know that my mother is very tender-hearted. I slip the piece of paper into her missal, in order to frighten her and thus soften her up, with the intention of coming back the next day to ask her for the necessary sum, in the hope of finding her more sympathetic. . . .

"But there's the second hypothesis. Why shouldn't I, too, want to kill her?

"Not all the Saint-Fiacre fortune has gone. There's a little money left. And in my position a little money, however little, may make all the difference.

"I am vaguely aware that Métayer is mentioned in the will. But a murderer can't inherit. . . .

"Isn't he the man everyone will suspect of the crime? He who spends part of his time at a printer's in Moulins? He who, living in the chateau, can slip the piece of paper into the missal whenever he likes?

"Didn't I arrive at Moulins on Saturday afternoon? And didn't I wait there with my mistress for the result of this operation?"

He stood up, his glass in his hand.

"Your good health, gentlemen! . . . You look gloomy. The whole of my mother's poor life these last few years was gloomy. . . . Isn't that so, Father? . . . It's only fair that her last night should be accompanied by a little gaiety."

He looked the chief inspector straight in the eyes.

"Your good health, Monsieur Maigret!"

He was making fun of somebody, but of whom? Of himself? Of everybody else?

Maigret felt that he was confronted by a force against which there was nothing to be done. Certain individuals, at a given moment in their lives, have an hour of fulfilment like this, an hour during which they are, as it were, situated above the rest of mankind and above themselves.

Such is the case of the gambler who, at Monte Carlo, wins all the time, whatever he does. Such is the case of the hitherto unknown member of the opposition who, with a speech he makes, brings down the government, and is the first to be surprised, since all he wanted was a few lines in the official record.

Maurice de Saint-Fiacre was living this hour. There was a strength in him that he had never before guessed he had, and the others could do nothing but bow their heads.

But wasn't it drink that was carrying him away like this?

"Let's go back to the starting point of our conversation, gentlemen, seeing that it isn't midnight yet. . . . I have said that my mother's murderer is here among us. I have proved that he could be I or any one of you, except, perhaps, the chief inspector and the doctor.

"I'm not even sure of that. . . .

"And I have prophesied his death. . . .

"Will you allow me to play the hypothesis game once again? He knows that the law is powerless against him. But he also knows that there are, or will be, a few persons, six at least, who know about his crime. . . .

"There, again, we are faced with several solutions. . . .

"The first is the most romantic, the most consistent with the spirit of Walter Scott.

172

"But here I must open a fresh parenthesis. What is the distinguishing feature of this crime? It is that there are at least five individuals who were revolving around the countess . . . five individuals who stood to benefit by her death, each of whom may have envisaged the means of bringing about that death. . . .

"Only one dared. Only one killed.

"Well, gentlemen, I can easily imagine that individual taking advantage of this dinner party to revenge himself on the others. He is done for! Why not get rid of all of us?"

And Maurice de Saint-Fiacre, with a disarming smile, looked at each guest in turn.

"Isn't it fascinating? The dining room of the old chateau, the candles, the table loaded with bottles . . . Then, at midnight, death . . . You will note that at the same time all possibility of scandal would be averted. Tomorrow, people would find us and be completely baffled. They would talk of an accident, or of a terrorist plot."

The lawyer stirred on his chair and anxiously glanced around, into the darkness that began less than a yard from the table.

"If I may venture to recall that I am a doctor," growled Bouchardon, "I would recommend a cup of strong black coffee for everybody."

"And I," the priest said slowly, "would remind you that there is a dead person in the house."

Saint-Fiacre hesitated for a moment. A foot brushed against Maigret's ankle, and he bent down quickly, but once again too late.

"I asked you to give me until midnight. I have only examined the first hypothesis. There is another. . . . The murderer, hunted down, panic-stricken, blows out his brains. . . . *But I don't think he will do that.*"

"For God's sake let's go into the smoking room!" yelped the lawyer, standing up and hanging on to the back of his chair to avoid falling.

"Finally, there is a third hypothesis. Somebody who cares for the honor of the family comes to the murderer's help. Wait a moment . . . The question is more complicated than that. Mustn't a scandal be avoided at all costs? Shouldn't the culprit be *helped* to commit suicide?

"The revolver is there, gentlemen, at an equal distance from every hand. . . . It is ten minutes to twelve. . . . I repeat that at midnight the murderer will be dead."

And this time he spoke so emphatically that nobody said a word. Everyone held his breath.

"The victim is up there, watched over by

a servant. . . . The murderer is here, surrounded by seven people. . . ."

The count drained his glass, and the anonymous foot continued to brush against Maigret's.

"Six minutes to twelve . . . Isn't this just like Walter Scott? I trust the murderer is beginning to shake in his shoes."

He was drunk, but he went on drinking.

"Five people at least with reason to rob an old woman deprived of her husband and starved for love . . . Only one who dared . . . It will be a bomb or a revolver, gentlemen. A bomb that will blow us all up, or a revolver that will kill only the culprit. . . . Four minutes to twelve . . ."

Then he added in a curt voice:

"Don't forget that nobody knows!"

He seized the bottle of whisky and served everybody, beginning with Maigret's glass and finishing with Emile Gautier's.

He did not fill his own. Hadn't he drunk enough? One candle went out. The others were on the point of following suit.

"I said midnight. . . . Three minutes to twelve . . ."

He was talking like an auctioneer.

"Three minutes to twelve . . . The murderer is going to die. You can begin saying your prayer, Father. As for you, Doctor, I trust you've brought your bag with you? . . . Two minutes to twelve . . . One and a half minutes . . ."

And all the time that insistent foot against Maigret's foot. He did not dare bend down again, for fear of missing something.

"I'm off!" exclaimed the lawyer.

All eyes turned toward him. He was standing, still gripping the back of his chair. He hesitated about venturing on the three dangerous steps that would take him to the door. He hiccuped.

And at the same moment a shot rang out. There was one second, perhaps two, of general immobility.

A second candle went out, and at the same time Maurice de Saint-Fiacre swayed, hit the back of his Gothic chair with his shoulders, leaned to the right, tried to regain his balance, but slumped to the floor in an inert mass, with his head against the priest's arm.

— 10 —

The Funeral Wake

The scene that followed was pure confusion. Something was happening everywhere, and afterward nobody could have described anything but the small part of the events he had seen himself.

Only five candles were left to light the whole dining room. Huge areas remained in darkness, and, as they moved about, people walked in and out of them as if they were the wings of a theater.

The man who had fired was one of Maigret's neighbors: Emile Gautier. And the shot had scarcely rung out, it seemed, before he was holding his wrists out toward the chief inspector in a rather theatrical gesture.

Maigret was standing. Gautier got up. His father did too. And the three of them formed a group on one side of the table, while another group gathered around the victim.

Count de Saint-Fiacre was still lying with his forehead against the priest's arm. The doctor had bent down and then looked around him with a grim expression.

"Is he dead?" asked the plump lawyer.

No reply. It was as if, in that group, the action was being played out limply by bad actors.

And there was Jean Métayer, who belonged to neither group. He had remained by his chair, trembling, uneasy. He did not know where to look.

During the minutes just before his action, Emile Gautier must have decided what attitude to adopt. After putting the weapon back on the table, and offering his wrists, he made a declaration, looking Maigret straight in the eyes.

"He said what was going to happen himself, didn't he? . . . The murderer had to die. And since he was too cowardly to do justice to himself . . ."

His self-assurance was extraordinary.

"I did what I considered to be my duty."

Could those on the other side of the table hear? There were footsteps in the hallway. It was the servants. The doctor went to the door to prevent them from coming in. Maigret did not hear what he said to get rid of them.

"I saw Saint-Fiacre prowling around the chateau on the night before the crime. . . . That was how I knew . . ."

The whole scene was badly organized. And Gautier was hamming badly when he declared:

"The judges will say whether . . ."

The doctor's voice could be heard asking:

"You're sure that it was Saint-Fiacre who killed his mother?"

"Positive! Would I have done what I've done if . . ."

"You saw him prowling around the chateau on the night before the crime?"

"I saw him as clearly as I can see you now. He had left his car just outside the village . . ."

"You have no other proof?"

"Yes, I have. This afternoon the altar boy came to see me at the bank with his mother. . . . It was his mother who made him talk. Shortly after the crime, the count asked the boy to give him the missal and promised him some money. . . ."

Maigret's patience was nearly exhausted; he felt he had been left out of the play.

Yes, a play! Why was the doctor smiling into his beard? And why was the priest gently pushing Saint-Fiacre's head away?

A play, moreover, that was to continue on a note of farce and serious drama combined.

Because Count de Saint-Fiacre was standing up like a man who had just had a nap. The expression in his eyes was hard, and there was an ironic but threatening crease at the corner of his mouth.

"Come here and say that again!" he said.

The cry that rang out was bloodcurdling. Emile Gautier was screaming with fear and hanging on to Maigret's arm, as if to ask him for protection. But the chief inspector drew back, leaving the field clear for the two men.

There was somebody who did not understand: Jean Métayer. And he was almost as frightened as the bank clerk.

To cap everything, the candelabrum fell over, and the tablecloth started smoldering, giving off a strong smell of burning. It was the lawyer who prevented the fire from taking hold, by emptying a bottle of wine over it.

"Come here!"

It was an order. And the tone in which it was given was such that they all knew there was no disobeying it.

Maigret had seized the revolver. A single glance had shown him that it was loaded with blanks.

The rest he could guess. Maurice de Saint-Fiacre letting his head fall against the priest's arm . . . A few whispered words asking for the illusion of his death to be preserved for a moment . . .

Now he was no longer the same man. He seemed taller, sturdier. He did not take his eyes off young Gautier, and it was the manager who suddenly ran toward a window, opened it, and shouted to his son:

"This way!"

It was not a bad plan. The confusion and excitement were so great at that moment that Gautier would have had a good chance of making his escape.

Did the little lawyer do it on purpose? Probably not. Or else it was drunkenness that invested him with a sort of heroism. As the fugitive was making for the window, he stretched out one leg, and Gautier fell headlong.

He did not get up by himself. A hand seized him by the collar, lifted him up and put him on his feet. He screamed again when he saw that it was Saint-Fiacre who was forcing him to stay upright.

"Don't move! . . . Somebody shut the window. . . ."

Then he slammed his fist into his companion's face, which turned crimson. He did it coldly.

"Now talk! . . . Tell us all about it . . ."

Nobody intervened. Nobody even thought

181

of doing so, they were so convinced that only one man had the right to raise his voice.

There was only old Gautier to growl in Maigret's ear:

"Are you going to let him do as he likes?"

Yes, he was! Maurice de Saint-Fiacre was in command of the situation, and he was adequate to his task.

"You saw me on the night in question, that's true enough."

Then he said to the others:

"Do you know where? . . . On the steps. I was going in. He was coming out. I was planning to take some of the family jewels to sell. We found ourselves face to face in the dark. It was freezing. And this little swine told me that he had just come from . . . Have you guessed? Yes, from my mother's bedroom!"

In a lower voice he added casually:

"I abandoned my plan. I went back to Moulins."

Jean Métayer had opened his eyes wide. The lawyer was stroking his chin nervously, and he kept glancing toward his glass but did not dare go and get it.

"That wasn't proof enough. There were two of them in the house, and Gautier could have been telling the truth. As I explained before, he was the first to take advantage of an old woman's unhappiness. Métayer only came along later. . . . Perhaps Métayer, conscious that his position was threatened, attempted to take his revenge. I tried to find out. Both of them were on their guard. It was as if they were defying me to do anything. . . ."

"That's true, isn't it, Gautier? . . . I was the gentleman with the bad checks who prowled around the chateau at night, and who wouldn't dare make any accusations, for fear of getting arrested himself. . . ."

In another tone of voice, he went on:

"Forgive me, Father, and you, too, Doctor, for inflicting all this filth on you. But, as we've already been told, real justice, the justice of the courts, is powerless here. . . . That's so, isn't it, Monsieur Maigret? . . . Did you understand, at least, when I was kicking you under the table just now?"

He was walking up and down, passing from the light into the shadows and from the shadows into the light. He was a man holding himself back, managing to remain calm only at the cost of a tremendous effort. Sometimes he went close enough to Gautier to touch him.

"What a temptation to pick up the revolver and fire! Yes, I had said myself that the culprit would die at midnight, and you

. . . you became the defender of the honor of the Saint-Fiacres."

This time his fist struck so hard, right in the middle of his face, that the bank clerk's nose began bleeding profusely.

Emile Gautier had the eyes of a dying animal. He reeled under the blow and looked as if he was on the point of weeping with pain, fear, and panic.

The lawyer tried to intervene, but Saint-Fiacre pushed him away.

"*You* keep out of this!"

And that "*you*" emphasized the enormous distance that separated them. Maurice de Saint-Fiacre dominated the company.

"Excuse me, gentlemen, but I have another little formality to see to."

He opened the door wide and turned toward Gautier.

"Come!"

The other stood rooted to the ground. The hallway was in darkness. He did not want to go out there with his adversary.

It did not take long. Saint-Fiacre went up to him and hit him again, so hard that he was knocked headlong into the hallway.

"Up there!"

He pointed to the staircase leading to the floor above.

"Chief Inspector, I warn you that . . ."

panted the manager.

The priest had turned his head away. He was suffering. But he did not have the strength to intervene. Everyone was at the end of his tether. Métayer poured himself a drink, not caring what it was, he was so parched.

"Where are they going?" asked the lawyer.

They could hear them walking along the hallway; the flagstones rang with the sound of their footsteps. And they could hear Gautier panting for breath.

"You knew everything," Maigret said slowly, in a very low voice, to the manager. "You were working hand in glove, you and your son! You already had the farms, the mortgages. . . . But Métayer remained a risk. So you decided to kill the countess, and at the same time get rid of the gigolo, who would fall under suspicion . . ."

A cry of pain. The doctor went into the corridor to see what was happening.

"It's nothing," he said. "The little swine doesn't want to go upstairs and he's being helped along."

"This is a scandal! It's a crime! . . . What is he going to do?" cried old Gautier, rushing out of the room.

Maigret and the doctor followed him. They arrived at the foot of the staircase just as the other two, upstairs, reached the door of the dead woman's bedroom.

And they heard Saint-Fiacre's voice:

"In you go!"

"I can't. . . . I . . ."

"In you go!"

A dull thud. Another blow.

Old Gautier ran up the stairs, followed by Maigret and Bouchardon. They arrived at the top just as the door was closing.

At first they could hear nothing behind the heavy oak door. The manager held his breath, grimacing in the dark.

A thin ray of light shone under the door.

"On your knees!"

A pause. A hoarse gasp.

"Quicker than that! . . . On your knees! . . . And now beg her forgiveness!"

Again, silence, which was very prolonged. A cry of pain. This time it was not a punch the murderer had received, but a kick full in the face.

"For . . . forgive me."

"Is that all? Is that all you can find to say? . . . Remember that it was she who paid for your studies . . ."

"Forgive me!"

"Remember that three days ago she was alive."

"Forgive me!"

"Remember, you dirty little swine, that you once wormed your way into her bed."

"Forgive me! . . . Forgive me!"

"You can do better than that! . . . Come, now. Tell her you are a filthy louse. . . . Repeat after me . . ."

"I am . . ."

"On your knees, I said! . . . Do you need a carpet?"

"Don't! . . . I . . ."

"Beg her forgiveness."

Suddenly these exchanges, which were separated by long silences, were followed by a series of loud noises. Saint-Fiacre had lost his self-control. There were a number of thuds.

Maigret opened the door a little. Saint-Fiacre was holding Gautier by the neck and banging his head on the floor.

When he saw the chief inspector, he let go, wiped his forehead, and straightened up.

"I've finished," he said, breathing fast.

He caught sight of the manager and frowned.

"Don't you feel the need to beg her forgiveness too?"

The old man was so frightened that he threw himself on his knees.

All they could see of the dead woman, in the light from a couple of tapers, was the nose, which seemed enormous, and the folded hands, which were holding a rosary.

"Get out!"

The count pushed the Gautiers out of the room and shut the door. The group started going downstairs.

Emile was bleeding. He could not find his handkerchief. The doctor passed him his.

The bank clerk was a horrible sight: a battered, bloodstained face, the nose nothing but a tumor and the upper lip split open.

And yet the ugliest, the most horrible thing about his appearance was the eyes, their shifty expression.

Maurice de Saint-Fiacre, very upright, like the master of a house who knows what he has to do, strode down the long ground-floor hallway and opened the door, letting in a gust of icy air.

"Get out!" he growled, turning toward the father and son.

But just as Emile was going out, he caught hold of him, with an instinctive gesture.

Maigret was certain that he heard a sob in the count's throat as he started hitting the bank clerk again, convulsively, and crying:

"You swine! You swine!"

It was enough for the chief inspector just to touch him on the shoulder. Saint-Fiacre regained his composure, literally threw the body down the steps, and shut the door.

But not before they had heard the old man's voice again:

"Emile? Where are you?"

The priest was praying, with his elbows on the sideboard. In one corner Métayer and his lawyer were sitting motionless, their eyes fixed on the door.

Maurice de Saint-Fiacre came in, his head held high.

"Gentlemen," he began.

But he could not go on. His voice was choked by emotion. He was at the end of his tether.

He shook hands with the doctor and Maigret, as much as to say they could now go. Then, turning toward Métayer and his companion, he waited.

Those two did not seem to understand. Or else they were paralyzed by fear.

To show them the way, a gesture was required, followed by a snap of the fingers.

That was all.

Or was it? The lawyer started looking for his hat, and Saint-Fiacre groaned:

"Quicker than that!"

Maigret heard a murmur of voices behind a door, and he guessed that it was the servants, trying to figure out what was happening in the chateau.

He put on his heavy overcoat. He felt the need to shake hands once more with Saint-Fiacre.

The door was open. Outside, it was a bright, cold night, without a single cloud. The poplars stood out against a moonlit sky. Footsteps rang out somewhere, a long way away. And there were lights in the windows of the manager's house.

"No, you stay, Father."

And, in the echoing hall, Maurice de Saint-Fiacre's voice added:

"Now, if you are not too tired, we are going to keep watch over my mother. . . ."

— *11* —
The Whistle

"You mustn't be cross with me, Monsieur Maigret, for looking after you so badly. . . . But, what with the funeral . . ."

Poor Marie Tatin was bustling around, getting whole crates of beer and lemonade ready.

"Especially seeing that those who live a long way off will drop in here for a bite . . ."

The fields were white with frost, and the grass crackled underfoot. Every quarter of an hour the passing bell of the little church tolled.

The hearse had arrived at dawn, and the undertaker's men were waiting at the inn, in a half-circle around the stove.

"I'm surprised the manager isn't at home," Marie Tatin had told them. "He's probably at the chateau with Monsieur Maurice. . . ."

Already a few peasants, who had put on their Sunday clothes, could be seen.

Maigret was finishing his breakfast when, through the window, he saw the altar boy arrive, holding his mother's hand. But the woman did not accompany him as far as the inn. She stopped at the corner of the road, where she thought she was out of sight, and pushed her son forward, as if to give him the necessary impetus to reach Marie Tatin's inn.

When Ernest came in, he was very self-assured, like a boy at school ready to recite a fable he has been rehearsing for three months.

"Is the chief inspector here?"

At the very moment he was asking Marie Tatin this question, he caught sight of Maigret and went toward him with his hands in his pockets, one of them toying with something.

"I've come to . . ."

"Show me your whistle."

Ernest promptly took a step back, turned his eyes away, thought for a moment, and murmured:

"What whistle?"

"The one you've got in your pocket. Have you been wanting a scout whistle for a long time?"

The boy automatically took it from his pocket and put it on the table.

"Now tell me your little story."

A suspicious glance, followed by an imperceptible shrug of the shoulders. For Ernest was already cunning. The expression in his eyes said clearly:

"I don't care! I've got the whistle! I'm going to say what I was told to say."

And he recited:

"It's about the missal. . . . I didn't tell you everything the other day, because I was scared of you. . . . But Ma wants me to tell the truth. . . . Somebody came and asked me for the missal, just before High Mass. . . ."

All the same, he was red in the face, and he snatched the whistle back as if he were afraid of having it confiscated because of his lie.

"And who came and asked you for it?"

"Monsieur Métayer . . . The secretary at the chateau . . ."

"Come and sit next to me. . . . Would you like a grenadine?"

"Yes. With fizzy water."

"Bring us a grenadine with soda water, Marie. . . . And you, are you pleased with your whistle? . . . Blow it for me."

The undertaker's men turned around when they heard the whistle.

"Your mother bought it for you yesterday afternoon, didn't she?"

"How do you know?"

"How much did they give her yesterday at the bank?"

The boy looked him in the eyes. He was no longer red in the face, but pale. He glanced toward the door, as if to see how far he was from it.

"Drink your grenadine . . . It was Emile Gautier who saw you. He taught you what to say."

"Yes!"

"He told you to accuse Jean Métayer?"

"Yes."

And, after a pause for thought:

"What are you going to do to me?"

Maigret forgot to reply. He was thinking. He was thinking that his part in this case had been limited to finding the last link, a tiny link that completed the chain.

It was Jean Métayer, all right, whom Gautier had wanted to have accused. But events of the previous evening had upset his plans. He had realized that the man he had to fear was not the secretary, but Count de Saint-Fiacre.

If all had gone well, he would have been obliged to go to see the red-haired boy again before long, to teach him a new lesson:

"You must say that it was Monsieur the Count who asked you for the missal. . ."

And now the boy repeated:

"What are you going to do to me?"

Maigret did not have time to reply. The lawyer came down the stairs, entered the main room of the inn, and approached Maigret, his hand outstretched, with a hint of hesitation.

"Did you sleep well, Chief Inspector? . . . Excuse me . . . I would like to ask your advice, on behalf of my client. . . . I have such a terrible headache. . . ."

He sat down, or, rather, slumped on the bench.

"The funeral is at ten o'clock, isn't it?"

He looked at the undertaker's men, then at the people passing along the road, waiting for the funeral to begin.

"Between us, do you think that Métayer's duty is to . . . Don't misunderstand me. We know the situation, and it's precisely out of a sense of delicacy that . . ."

"Can I go now, monsieur?"

Maigret did not hear. He was listening to the lawyer.

"Haven't you understood yet?"

"I mean if one examines . . ."

"Let me give you a piece of advice: Don't examine anything at all!"

"In your opinion it would be better to leave without . . ."

Too late! Ernest, who had his whistle safe

195

in his pocket, had opened the door and taken to his heels.

"From the legal point of view, we are in an excellent position . . ."

"Yes, excellent!"

"Isn't it? . . . That's what I was saying to . . ."

"Did he sleep well?"

"He didn't even undress. He's a very high-strung, very sensitive fellow, like many young men of good family, and . . ."

But the undertaker's men were pricking up their ears, standing up, paying for their drinks. Maigret stood up too, took his coat with the velvet collar from the stand, and wiped his bowler hat with his sleeve.

"The two of you have a chance to slip away during . . ."

"During the funeral? . . . In that case, I must telephone for a taxi."

"That's right."

The priest was in his surplice, Ernest and two other altar boys in their black cassocks. The cross was carried by a priest from a nearby village, who was walking fast because of the cold. They were intoning liturgical chants as they hurried along the road.

The peasants were grouped at the foot

of the steps. Nothing could be seen inside. Finally the door opened and the coffin appeared, carried by four men.

Behind was a tall silhouette: Maurice de Saint-Fiacre, red-eyed, very erect.

He was not in black. He was the only person not wearing mourning.

And yet, when, from the top of the steps, he let his gaze wander over the crowd, there was a feeling of embarrassment.

He came out of the chateau with no one beside him. And he followed the coffin alone.

From where he stood, Maigret could see the manager's house, which had been his own home. The doors and windows were closed.

The shutters of the chateau were closed too. Only in the kitchen could some servants be seen, their noses pressed against the windowpanes.

The sound of the sacred chants was almost drowned by the crunch of footsteps on the gravel.

The bell was in full peal.

Two pairs of eyes met: the count's and Maigret's.

Was the chief inspector mistaken? It seemed to him that Maurice de Saint-Fiacre's lips were touched by the ghost of a smile.

Not the smile of the skeptical Parisian, the penniless prodigal.

A serene, confident smile . . .

During the Mass, everybody heard the high-pitched horn of a taxi. A little swine was making his escape in the company of a lawyer with a hangover.

The employees of THORNDIKE PRESS hope you have enjoyed this Large Print book. All our Large Print books are designed for easy reading — and they're made to last.

Other Thorndike Large Print books are available at your library, through selected bookstores, or directly from us. Suggestions for books you would like to see in Large Print are always welcome.

For more information about current and upcoming titles, please call or mail your name and address to:

THORNDIKE PRESS
PO Box 159
Thorndike, Maine 04986
800/223-6121
207/948-2962